Max

A pain like none she'd experienced sliced through Cammi's midsection.

Reid was on his feet and beside her in a heartbeat. "What's the matter?"

Try as she might, Cammi couldn't find her voice. Squeezing her eyes shut, she gripped her stomach and prayed. *Not the baby, Lord. Please don't let it be the baby....*

"Georgia," Reid bellowed to the diner owner as he scooped Cammi up in his powerful arms, "call the emergency room. Tell them we're on the way."

"Don't look so scared, pretty lady," he said after he gently deposited her inside his truck and buckled the seat belt. "Everything will be all right."

Leaning against the headrest, she closed her eyes. *Stay calm*, she told herself. *The Father is with you.*

Reid reached across the seat to squeeze her hand. "Keep a good thought, okay?"

"Pray, Reid," she managed to say. "Please...pray for me...."

Books by Loree Lough

Love Inspired

Suddenly Daddy #28
Suddenly Mommy #34
Suddenly Married #52
Suddenly Reunited #107
Suddenly Home #130
His Healing Touch #163
Out of the Shadows #179
†*An Accidental Hero* #214

*Suddenly!
†Accidental Blessings

LOREE LOUGH

A full-time writer for many years, Loree Lough has produced more than 2,000 articles, dozens of short stories and novels for the young (and young at heart), and all have been published here and abroad. The award-winning author of more than thirty-five romances, Loree also writes as Cara McCormack and Aleesha Carter.

A comedic teacher and conference speaker, Loree loves sharing in classrooms what she's learned the hard way. The mother of two grown daughters, she lives in Maryland with her husband and an old-as-dirt cat named Mouser (who, until recently—when she caught and killed her first mouse—had no idea what a rodent was).

AN
ACCIDENTAL
HERO

LOREE LOUGH

Published by Steeple Hill Books™

STEEPLE HILL BOOKS

Steeple
Hill™

ISBN 0-373-87221-6

AN ACCIDENTAL HERO

Visit us at www.steeplehill.com

Printed in U.S.A.

...wait on the Lord, and He shall save thee.
—*Proverbs* 20:22

To my family,
whose loving support gives me courage, and to the
heroes who save us from all manner of danger
without a second thought for themselves,
for *that* is true courage.

Chapter One

Cammi Carlisle had been heading east on Route 40 since dawn, doing her level best to keep her mind on the road rather than the reasons she'd left Los Angeles. It would take Herculean strength and the courage of Job, too, to tell her father everything she'd done since moving away from Texas....

Sighing, she looked away from the rain-streaked windshield long enough to glance at the blue-green numerals on her dashboard clock. Fifteen minutes, tops, and she'd be home. Dread settled over her like an itchy blanket.

Her dad would never come right out and voice his disapproval of her decisions. Instead, he'd shake his head and say, "It's your life...but I think you'll be sorry...."

He'd said it when she signed up for Art instead of Bookkeeping in high school, when she traded her scholarship to Texas U. for acting lessons at the community college, when she announced her plans to move to Hollywood and try her hand at acting.

Cammi sighed, wondering how old she'd have to be before her dad no longer made her feel like a knobby-kneed, silly little—

From out of nowhere, came the angry blare of a car horn, the *whoosh-hiss* of tires skidding on rain-slicked pavement, the deafening impact of metal smashing into metal…. Then came an instant of utter stillness, punctuated by the soft tinkling of broken glass peppering the blacktop.

Cammi loosened her grip on the steering wheel and took stock. She'd been traveling north, but her fifteen-year-old coupe now faced south in the intersection of Amarillo's Western Avenue and Plains Boulevard— the very corner where, thirteen years earlier, on a rainy night much like this one, her mother had died in a fiery car wreck.

Still reeling from the shock of the impact, Cammi stepped shakily onto the pavement. She didn't seem to be hurt, and prayed whoever was in the other car had been as fortunate. Not much hope of that, though—the vehicle reminded her more of a modern-art sculpture than a pickup.

The truck's side window had shattered on impact, making it impossible to see the driver. Gently, she rapped on the crystallized glass. "Hello…hello? Are you all right in there?"

"I'm fine, no thanks to you," came the gruff reply.

The door slowly opened with a loud, protesting groan. One pointy-toed cowboy boot thumped to the ground, immediately followed by the other.

"Are you *crazy?*" the driver demanded as he stood and faced her.

Pedestrians had gathered on the street corners as the drivers of other vehicles leaned out of their car windows: "Anyone hurt?" one woman asked.

"Doesn't appear so," a male voice answered, "but I'm gonna be late, thanks to these idiots...."

Good grief, Cammi thought. As if her reasons for coming home weren't bad enough, now she'd have to add "caused a car crash, smack-dab in the middle of town" to the already too-long list. Suddenly, she felt light-headed and grabbed the gnarled fender of the cowboy's pickup for support. He waved back the small crowd that had gathered, and steadied her, two strong hands gripping her upper arms. Crouching slightly, he squinted and stared into her eyes.

"You okay? Should I call 911?"

The dizziness passed as quickly as it had descended. Cammi shook her head. "No. I'm okay." And to prove it, she stepped away from his truck and smiled.

He thumbed his Stetson to the back of his head and looked her over from head to toe. Satisfied Cammi was indeed all right, he nodded and crossed both arms over his chest. "Did you even *see* that red light?"

Blinking as the cold October rain sheeted down her cheeks, she stared, slack-jawed and silent, as her gaze slid from his dark, frowning eyebrows to his full-lipped, scolding mouth. Not a bump or bruise, Cammi noted, not so much as a split lip. Thank God for that! "I-I'm sorry. I don't know what was..."

He ignored her just as surely as he ignored the

quickly thinning crowd. Muttering under his breath, he began pacing circles around what was left of their vehicles. *"Is she blind?"* he said, throwing both hands into the air. "Where'd she get her driver's license, in a bubble gum machine?"

Unlike her sisters and so many of her friends, Cammi had earned her license on the first try, and hadn't been involved in so much as a fender bender since. "I can see perfectly well, thank you," she snapped, "and there isn't a thing wrong with my hearing, either."

He looked up suddenly. Scrubbing both hands over his face, he expelled a deep sigh, then slid a cell phone from his jacket pocket. "Well," he said, flipping it open and punching the keys with his forefinger, "at least you're not hurt." Frowning, he gave her a second once-over.

If Cammi didn't know better, she'd have to say he looked downright concerned.

"You *are* all right, right?"

Except for that brief dizzy spell.—and Cammi thought she knew what was to blame for *that*—she'd come through the accident unharmed. A quick nod was her answer.

Facing the intersection, he spoke quietly into the phone, shaking his head. He reminded her a bit of her father, what with his frustrated gestures and matter-of-fact reporting of the facts. He probably outweighed her dad by twenty pounds, all of it muscle, she decided, remembering the way his strong hands had steadied her moments earlier. The similarities made Cammi swallow, hard, knowing that the reprimand this cowboy gave her would pale when compared to the look of disapproval she'd see in her father's eyes once she got home. It would've been tough enough, bringing him up to speed on the reasons she'd left L.A.—*without* this mess. Especially one so similar to the wreck that killed her mother. Especially considering that in his mind, this too, like so many other things, had been her fault.

Stubborn determination, she knew, was the only thing that stood between her and tears. But there'd be plenty of time for self-pity later, after she'd told her father about Rusty, about the—

"Tow trucks are on the way," he said, interrupting her reverie. He snapped his phone shut, dropped it back into his pocket. "You look a little green around the gills," he added, wrapping those big fingers around her upper arm yet again. "Soakin' wet, too," he continued, leading her toward Georgia's Diner. And in a voice she couldn't describe as anything but tender, he added, "What-say you wait inside, where it's warm and dry, while I take care of things out here."

She hated to admit it, but she *did* feel a bit dazed and confused. Why else would she have so quickly and willingly followed his instructions?

As he reached for the door handle, Cammi considered the possibility that he was one of those multiple personality types…raging mad one minute, sweet as honey the next. What if he'd just robbed a bank, and the accident had interfered with his getaway?

He held the door open and smiled. "Order me a cup of coffee, will ya?" He nodded toward the intersection. "I have a feeling I'm gonna need it once that mess is cleaned up."

Like a windup doll, Cammi went where he'd aimed her, wondering yet again why she was being so agreeable. It wasn't like her to let others tell her what to do. She chalked it up to the welcoming comfort of being in the restaurant where, as a teenager, she'd spent hundreds of hours, earning spending money for movies and mascara and the myriad of other things high school girls need.

"Hey, Georgia," Cammi said, stepping behind the counter to grab the coffeepot. "Mind if I help myself?"

"Well, as I live and breathe!" Cammi's former boss tossed her cleaning rag aside to add, "Look what the wind blew in!" Georgia wrapped Cammi in a warm hug, then held her at arm's length. "You sure are a sight for sore eyes, honey. Are y'home for a little visit? I'll bet your dad is just thrilled outta his socks. Every time that man comes in here, it's 'Cammi this' and 'Cammi that.'"

It stunned her a bit, hearing her father had spoken well of her. But Lamont London had never been one to air his dirty laundry in public. She waited for Georgia to take a breath. "I'm home to stay," she managed to say between hugs. "Had a little accident out there in the intersection, and that's why I'm—"

"Accident? You okay, honey?" Georgia pressed chubby palms to Cammi's cheeks. "Let's have a look at you…."

Cammi gave Georgia a one-armed hug, mindful of the hot coffee sloshing in the egg-shaped pot she held in her other hand. "I'm fine, but my car isn't. And neither is that cowboy's pickup truck." She took a step back and pointed toward the intersection. "I was told to wait in here while he 'took care of business.'"

"Well, now, will wonders never cease. A real-live gentleman, in this day and age!" Georgia walked toward the customer who'd just seated himself at the counter. "Glad to have you home, honey," she said, winking at Cammi. "You know where ever'thing is, so go right ahead and help yourself."

Cammi filled two mugs with coffee and carried them to a booth near the window wall. The overhead lights glinted from the narrow gold band on the third finger of her left hand. Sighing, she stared through the diner's window, watching the cowboy "taking care of things" out there. For all she knew, he could be arranging to steal her car and everything in it. Why had she so casually handed over control of the situation, when usually, *she* demanded to be in charge of her life?

Cammi groaned softly, knowing that wasn't even remotely true. No one in charge of her own life could have messed things up as badly as she had this time!

Maybe his soothing DJ-deep voice was the reason she'd obeyed like a well-programmed robot, or was it those greener-than-emeralds eyes? Or that slanted half smile? Or his soft Texas drawl...?

Fingernails drumming quietly on the tabletop, she sipped black coffee, watching as he talked with yellow-slickered police officers, as he scribbled on the tow truck drivers' clipboards, as he collected business cards. He pointed and gestured, nodded in a way she could only term *efficient*. No, she corrected, the better word was definitely *manly*.

Once both tow trucks drove off with their loads, he

headed for the diner, big shoulders hunched and hands pocketed as he plowed through wind and driving rain. It suddenly dawned on her that the coffee she'd poured for him would be cold by now. Cammi hurried to the counter for a hot refill, and was just settling back into the booth when he walked through the door.

He shook rain from his hat and denim jacket and hung them on the pole attached to the seat back, then slid onto the bench across from her. "I, uh, owe you an apology."

Not a word about the trouble he'd gone to out there, about being drenched by the cold rain, about being without his truck for who knows how long…thanks to her. Cammi blinked and, smiling a bit, held up one hand. "Wait, let me get this straight…*I* ran the red light, totaled your truck, and *you're* apologizing?"

His cheeks reddened and his brow furrowed. "Yeah, well, I went overboard. *Way* overboard." He wrapped both hands around his mug, then met her eyes. "Wasn't any need for me to get that hot under the collar."

She'd had plenty of time, sitting there alone, to toss a few ideas around in her head. His truck hadn't been a new model, and his clothes, though clean and neatly pressed, had a timeworn look to them. Which told her that, without his pickup he'd likely be hard-pressed for a way to get to work. No wonder he'd given her such a dressing-down! Now his quiet, grating voice and the haunted look in his eyes made her believe something far more serious than property damage had inspired his former grumpy mood.

"Let's make a deal," she suggested. "If the mechanic can get your truck back on the road in a day or two, *then* you can apologize for blowing things out of proportion." She grinned. "But I have a feeling that apology isn't going to be necessary, don't you?"

His smile never quite made it to his eyes, Cammi noted.

For an instant, she considered asking about that. Instead, she slid a paper napkin toward him. Earlier, she'd jotted her insurance agent's name and number and her own cell phone number on it. "Better drink up while it's hot," she said, pointing to his mug. Before he could agree or object, she tacked on, "I want to assure you the accident won't cost you a dime. It was my fault, completely, so if you need a rental car until your pickup is repaired, or if—"

His mouth formed a thin line when he interrupted. "Thanks, but I'll manage." He held out one hand and cleared his throat. "Name's Reid, by the way. Reid Alexander."

She wondered if his skin was naturally this warm, or had the hot coffee cup heated it? "Cammi Carlisle," she said. It still seemed strange, saying "Carlisle" instead of "London." Deep down, she admitted her new last name wouldn't upset her dad half as much as the rest of what she would have to tell—

"If you have a pen," Reid was saying, "I'll give you my phone number, too, in case your insurance agent needs it."

Cammi fished the felt-tip pen from her purse and watched as he plucked a napkin from the chrome stand-up holder on the windowsill. She liked the strong, sure lines of his handwriting, the firm way he gripped the pen. He had a nice face, too, open and honest, with look-straight-at-you green eyes that told her he was a good, decent man.

But then, she'd believed that about Rusty Carlisle, too…at first.

"Hungry?" he asked as she tucked his phone number into her purse.

She didn't think she'd ever seen thicker, darker lashes on a man. "As a matter of fact, I haven't had a bite all day."

He raised an arm and waved. "Hey, Georgia," he called, grinning. "How 'bout a couple menus over here."

The husky redhead shot a "you've gotta be kidding" look his way, and propped a fist on an ample hip. "I don't remember seeing you come in here on crutches, honey, so unless your leg is broken, come get 'em yourself." To Cammi, she mouthed *Men!* and went back stacking clean plates behind the counter.

Reid chuckled. "Be right back," he whispered. "Wouldn't want to rile the cook."

"Right," Cammi agreed, "'cause y'never know *what* might end up on your plate."

She liked the way he walked…like a man who knew who he was and where he was going in life. He leaned over the counter and grabbed two plastic-coated menus and exchanged a few words with Georgia. The good-natured tone of their banter told Cammi they knew one another well. Funny that Cammi didn't know him, too; she'd only been away from Amarillo two years, after all.

Only. A silent, bitter laugh echoed in her head. The

past twenty-four months seemed like a lifetime now....

When he returned, Reid slid into the booth, handed her one menu, flattened the other on the table in front of him. "So, what can I order you?"

Georgia made the best burgers in Texas and Cammi had been craving one of her specialties for weeks. "I'll have a bacon cheeseburger and fries, on one condition."

He met her gaze. "Condition?"

There was no mistaking the suspicion and mistrust written on his handsome face. Cammi wondered what—or *who*—had caused it. "I'm buying," she announced, holding up a hand to forestall his argument. "You'd be home now, safe and sound and chowing down something home-cooked, no doubt, if I hadn't plowed through that red light. Buying your supper is the least I can do, and I won't take no for an answer."

That teasing look on his face made Cammi's stomach lurch. Was he *flirting* with her? Under normal circumstances, she might have been flattered. But these were hardly normal circumstances.

"There isn't a nickel's worth of fight left in me. So okay, you'll buy, this time."

This time?

Cammi got to her feet. What better way to hide from her reaction than to put on her "efficient waitress" face? "A lifetime ago," she explained, "I worked here at Georgia's. Maybe I can pull a few strings, get you some extra fries or a free slice of pie." She wiggled her eyebrows. "Georgia bakes it herself, you know."

Laughing, Reid said, "Yeah, I know." Then he added, "I'll have whatever you're having."

Cammi hurried to the counter, and came back carrying silverware in one hand and a pitcher of ice water in the other. She was about to leave again, to get glasses and straws, when he grabbed her wrist.

"Thanks," he said, giving it a little squeeze. "This is right nice of you, especially after the way I behaved out there."

The bright fluorescent light had turned his eyes greener still. "You behaved like any normal person would under those conditions." She eased free of his grasp. "This is the least I can do."

She puttered behind the counter and caught up with Georgia as the diner owner slapped burgers onto the grill and dumped frozen fries into the deep fryer. She couldn't help wondering as she watched her former boss poke the meat patties with a corner of a metal spatula, why she hadn't experienced any of these heart-stopping, stomach lurching "first meeting" feelings with Rusty. Cammi shook her head.

But honestly! What business did she have feeling *anything!* Cammi blamed the long drive, the accident, the reasons she'd been forced to leave L.A. for her strong reaction to Reid. Finding out she was going to be a mother on the very day she'd become a widow would make any woman behave strangely, right?

When Cammi finally slid the food-laden tray onto their table, Reid gave an admiring nod. "It's like riding a bike," she said, dismissing his unspoken compliment, "you never forget how to balance." *If only balancing my* life *were as easy as balancing this tray,* she thought.

He waited until she was seated to say, "I owe you more than an apology, I owe you an explanation. All that bellowing and..." He shook his head. "Well, it was just plain uncalled for. This is a flimsy excuse, I know, but I had a similar experience some years back, and *that* accident..." He took a deep breath, exhaled. "Let's just say I'm downright sorry for behaving like a mule-headed fool."

His admission conjured a memory, one so strong Cammi didn't trust her voice. The boy who'd been driving the truck the night her mother died...*his* name had been Reid. One and the same? Or a queer coincidence?

She didn't realize how intently she'd been staring until he shifted uncomfortably in the seat. If he was *that* Reid....

"Did you know that cold fries cause indigestion?" she asked.

His expression said, *Huh?*

Using a French fry as a pointer, Cammi explained: "It has something to do with the way cooking oils mix with stomach acids. I think. Something like that." She was rambling and knew it, but better to have him think she was a babbling idiot than to press him for details...and find out she might be sitting face to face with the guy who'd killed her mother.

She'd been horrified to learn how her danger-hungry stuntman husband had died, but his death only served to underscore what she'd realized on their wedding night—they hadn't married for love. The cold hard fact was, they'd been friends with one thing in common: a tendency to act on impulse.

So jumping to conclusions about Reid didn't seem

the smartest thing to do at the moment. Besides, she recognized Reid's far-off expression as an attempt to hide from the miseries of his past. She recognized it because she felt exactly the same way. Cammi wanted to comfort him, if only for this brief moment in time, and gave in to the urge to blanket his fidgeting hands with hers.

Then, suddenly, for a reason she couldn't explain, Cammi found herself biting back tears, found herself feeling guilty for harboring so much anger toward Rusty. It would be hard, very hard, getting past the *way* her husband had died…and with whom. Still, on the day he'd been buried, Cammi had promised herself that Rusty's child would never know those awful details.

Reid eased his hands from beneath hers and broke the uneasy silence. "So, you live 'round these parts?"

She hadn't realized until that moment exactly how much she'd missed hearing a good old-fashioned Texas drawl, how much she'd missed Amarillo, how good it felt to be on familiar turf. "Actually," she said, shrugging, "my dad lives not too far from here." She sipped her soda. "And you?"

It seemed as if a shadow crossed his face, darkening his features.

Reid cleared his throat. "Once, I was a…" He took a deep breath and started over. "Well, I'm a ranch hand now."

He said "now" as if it were "the end," and she wondered for a moment why. But Cammi wouldn't ask that question, either, because crashing into his life had already caused enough damage, without rousing bad memories as well. From now on, she'd keep the conversation light, carefree, noncommittal.

Cammi looked out the window, gestured toward the bustling street. "I grew up in Amarillo, but I've been away a few years."

He smiled. "Lemme guess…you're married with kids, and your husband's job took you away from home."

"No." She stared into her mug, saw the overhead lights glimmering on the surface of the glossy black coffee. She could tell him about Rusty, about the rush wedding, but then she'd have to admit what an addle-brained twit she'd been, running off without a thought or a prayer to marry a man for no reason other than that he'd asked her to. "No husband, no kids." She pressed a palm to her stomach. *At least, no kids yet,* she thought. "I've been in California, trying to become an actress," she finished in a singsong voice.

Usually when she said that, people chuckled at her admission, rolled their eyes, smiled condescendingly. Cammi waited for one of the typical responses. It surprised her when instead, Reid said in a soft, raspy drawl, "Well, you're sure pretty enough to be a movie star."

Everything, from his smile to his tone to the sparkle in his eyes told her Reid was interested in her. If they'd met him at another time, under different circumstances…

But even if Cammi trusted her judgment—and considering the gravity and multitude of her mistakes, she most definitely did not—what man in his right mind would consciously get involved with a pregnant widow?

"So, what happened?" Reid asked.

"Happened?"

"To your acting career."

Thankfully, he hadn't asked about the *rest* of her life.

While she'd inherited her mother's dark eyes and hair, the acting-talent gene hadn't been passed down. Cammi had given it her all out there in L.A., but she'd had less luck pleasing directors than she'd had pleasing her dad. "Guess I just wasn't cut out for Hollywood," she said.

It was true, after all, in more ways than one: And when this pleasant little meal and friendly conversation ended, she'd have to go home and admit that fact—and a few more—to her father and sisters.

Home.

She glanced at her watch. "I'd better see about getting a taxi. My dad was expecting me over an hour ago. Don't want to worry him."

"I'd drive you, but..." He extended his hands in helpless supplication.

Cammi took no offense at the reference to his destroyed pickup because there hadn't been a trace of sarcasm in his voice. "You oughta smile more often." One brow lifted in response to her compliment, making him look even more handsome. Cammi felt the heat of a blush color her cheeks. "I like your smile, is all," she said, and started digging in her purse.

Reid leaned forward. "What're you looking for?"

The rummaging had been a good excuse to avert her gaze. "Change, for the pay phone." A half-truth was better than an outright lie, right? "My cell phone's dead." Cammi glanced toward the booth on the far wall and made a move to get up, but Reid held up a hand to stop her.

"Here," he said, passing her his cell phone. "I never use up all the minutes on my plan, anyway."

He sent her a lopsided grin that made her heart beat double time. She had no business reacting to this man. For one thing, he might well be partly responsible for her mother's death. For another, she was newly widowed…and with child.

"While you're at it, ask the dispatcher to send two cabs."

She flipped the phone open. "You wouldn't happen to have the number of the taxi company programmed into this thing, would you?"

"Never had any use for cabs, myself." On his feet, he added, "But I can duck into the phone booth over there and look one up." He grabbed the cell phone. "Might as well call 'em myself, long as I'm in there, anyway."

She watched him walk away. Reid was different from just about every man she'd met in California. Oh, he was good-looking enough to join the parade of those pounding the pavement in search of leading man roles—more than attractive enough to land a few, too. Which is why it seemed so strange that everything about him, from the leather of his cowboy boots to the top of his dark-haired head screamed "genuine."

Careful, Cammi, she warned. *The man doesn't need any more trouble in his life.*

And neither did she, for that matter.

Chapter Two

If he'd had the sense God gave a goose, Reid would have ordered Georgia's pie for dessert, or another cup of strong, diner coffee. He would have pretended that a ravenous appetite required yet another burger. Something, *any*thing to keep Cammi with him a little while longer. But once he'd called for the taxis, there was no stopping time, and Reid had to satisfy himself with hanging around as they waited for their drivers. For several minutes after hers drove off, he found himself staring as the taillights turned into glowing red pinpricks before disappearing into the rainy black night.

"Where's your truck?" Billy asked half an hour later, nodding toward the taxi that had delivered Reid to the Rockin' C Ranch.

He flung his jacket onto the hall tree. "Had a crack-up in town."

His friend's face crinkled with concern. "You okay?" he asked, one hand on Reid's shoulder.

"Yeah." Physically, he was fine. But something had happened to his head, to his heart, sitting with Cammi at Georgia's. She looked awfully familiar, but he couldn't for the life of him remember where, or if, they'd ever met. Something he'd have to think about long and hard before he saw her again.

"Whose fault was it?"

Reid heard the caution in Billy's question; his friend didn't want to wake any sleeping ghosts, and Reid appreciated that. "Hers."

Nodding, Billy headed down the hall toward the kitchen. "Put on a pot of decaf couple minutes ago. Martina made apple pie for dessert tonight. Join me?"

Though he'd wolfed down his burger and fries before downing two cups of coffee at Georgia's Diner, Reid said, "Hard to say no to anything Martina whips up."

While Billy sliced pie, Reid filled a mug for each of them. "Li'l gal ran a red light," he explained, grabbing two forks from the silverware drawer, "and I broadsided her."

Wincing, Billy whistled. He didn't say more. Didn't have to. He'd been there *that* night, too.

"Really, son, you okay?"

Reid nodded. "Yeah." Okay as the likes of him deserved to be, anyway.

"Just remember, this one wasn't your fault, either."

Billy had talked "fault" after meeting then fourteen-year-old Reid at the E.R. "I talked to the cops," he'd said on the drive back to the Rockin' C, "and they told me three eyewitnesses stated for the record that Rose London ran the red light." Then he'd reached across the front seat and grabbed Reid's sleeve. "Quit fiddlin' with the bandage, son, or you'll wear a scar on your forehead the rest of your days."

Reid half smiled at the memory, because ironically, the scar he wore now, in almost exactly the same spot, had been inflicted by a raging Brahma bull, not a car accident.

"Stop lookin' so glum," Billy was saying. "Just remember, the accident wasn't your fault."

He'd said pretty much the same thing all those years ago: *"You're not to blame for what happened to the London woman."*

True enough—Mrs. Lamont London had run a red light, same as Cammi Carlisle, and he'd plowed into the side of *her* car, too. However, assigning fault did nothing to ease Reid's guilt. Not then, not now. And Billy had bigger problems to worry about than traffic accidents, present or past, since his doctor's prognosis.

"Georgia says 'hey,'" Reid said, changing the subject. "Said she misses seeing you and Martina."

The fork hung loose in Billy's big hand. Absentmindedly, he shoved an apple slice around on his plate. "Gettin' harder and harder to drag my weary bones into town," he said on a heavy sigh. "Gettin' hard to drag 'em anywhere."

Reid knew Billy had never been one to wallow in self-pity, so it didn't surprise him when his longtime friend sat up straighter, as if regretting the admission, and cleared his throat.

"That list I gave you this morning was longer'n my forearm," Billy said. "When did you have time to stop at Georgia's?"

So much for changing the subject, Reid thought. "Accident happened in front of her diner." Cammi's pretty, smiling face flashed in Reid's mind. "We, uh, the other driver and I got all the particulars out of the way over burgers and fries."

Billy chuckled. "Ain't that just like you, to buy the kid a meal after she cracks up your only means of transportation."

Kid? He nearly laughed out loud, because Cammi Carlisle was more woman than any he'd seen since returning to Amarillo. More woman, in fact, than the dozens who routinely followed him around the rodeo circuit. Right now, she was the one sunny spot in his otherwise gloomy life. He was about to admit *she'd* insisted on paying for the food when Billy spoke.

"Amanda called." Using his chin as a pointer, he added, "I wrote her number over there, on the pad beside the phone."

Reid groaned inwardly at being forced to recall his last day with the tall willowy blonde who, despite his arm's-length interest in her, seemed determined to change his mind about "the two of them."

He thought of the afternoon, more than six months ago, when the surgeon gave Reid permission to leave the Albuquerque hospital. Amanda had been there…*again*. He hadn't wanted to hurt her, so he blamed his sour mood on the months of physical therapy that lay ahead of him. "Isn't fair to string you along while I recuperate," he'd said. "I need time, to make some hard choices about the future."

He realized now that his evasiveness had given her hope that, at the end of his "alone time," she'd be part of that future.

Reid strode across the room, saw from the area code that Amanda had been near Amarillo when she'd called. Shaking his head, he groaned again, this time aloud. First thing in the morning, he'd call her, invite her to breakfast, and set things straight.

"Well," Billy interrupted, getting to his feet with obvious difficulty. "Guess I'll drag my ol' bones up to bed." He started clearing the table.

"I'll take care of these."

Chuckling, Billy winked. "I was hopin' you'd say that." He limped toward the door, stopping in the hallway. "Don't be up all night, now, frettin' about that accident, y'hear? I know it roused some ugly memories, but thinkin' it to death won't change anything."

True enough. Still… "I'll turn in soon."

The look on Billy's face said he knew a fib when he heard one. "Don't forget, the new ranch hands start at first light."

Reid only nodded.

"G'night, son."

Billy had been the closest thing to a father Reid would ever know. Watching him suffer, watching him die, as he was now doing, was about the hardest thing Reid had ever done in his life. A tight knot of regret formed in Reid's throat, all but choking off his gruff "'Night."

He listened as Billy shuffled slowly up the steps. If he could trade his own robust health to get Billy's back, he'd do it in a heartbeat, because what did *he* have to live for, to look forward to? Sadly, life wasn't like that. Reid would have to be satisfied with doing

everything humanly possible to make Billy as comfortable as possible during the time he had left.

Standing woodenly, Reid gathered up the dishes
and added them to the already full dishwasher. The
fact that Martina hadn't turned it on told him that
she'd known her husband and ''adopted'' son would
share a late-night snack. The thought made him smile
a bit, despite the dark thoughts pricking at his memory.

The drone of the dishwasher's motor harmonized
with the ticking clock and the pinging of water in the
baseboard heaters. It wasn't really furnace weather
just yet, but because of Billy's steadily declining condition, Martina had set the thermostat at seventy de-
grees and left it there. The mere thought made Reid
wince. When his hot-tempered stepfather was diagnosed with cancer, it hadn't hurt like this—hearing
the news about Billy's condition had been painful and
terrifying. It didn't take a membership in Mensa to
figure out why; almost from the moment Reid set foot
on Rockin' C soil, Billy had scolded him for not doing his all-out best on chores, helped with homework,
convinced Reid he *was* good enough to ask the pret-
tiest girl on the cheerleading squad to the homecoming dance.

One palm resting on either side of the sink, Reid
stared out the kitchen window, watching raindrops
snake down the glass as wind buffeted Martina's but-
terfly bushes. She often stood here, overlooking the
wildlife that visited her gardens. She'd probably been
standing on this spot when she'd called him a couple
months back to tell him about Billy's prognosis.

After they hung up, Reid threw everything he

owned into his duffle bag and drove straight through, arriving in Amarillo the very next day. He'd moved into the same room he'd occupied when his mom was the Rockin' C housekeeper and his stepdad the foreman.

Hanging his head, Reid wondered if he would've been so quick to come back and help out if his injuries hadn't already ended his rodeo career.

Just one more thing to feel guilty about.

Well, he was here now. Determined to do everything in his power to help Billy and Martina, in any way he could, for as long as they needed him.

The grandfather clock in the hall struck one, reminding him that Billy was right: The rooster crowed mighty early at the Rockin' C. If Reid knew what was good for him, he'd try to catch some shut-eye, starting now. He flicked off the kitchen's overhead light and quietly climbed the wide, wooden stairs, skipping the third and the tenth so the predictable *squeak* wouldn't wake Billy or Martina.

Two hours later, he lay on his back, fingers linked beneath his head, still staring at the darkened ceiling. The rain had stopped, but the wind blew harder than ever, rattling the panes in his French doors.

He wondered if Cammi had made it home safely, if her homecoming had been warm and welcoming. She hadn't seemed at all that enthused about being back in Amarillo. Brokenhearted because she hadn't "made it" in Hollywood? Reid didn't think so. Cammi seemed too down-to-earth, too levelheaded for pie-in-the-sky dreams of stardom. No, her reluctance, he believed, was more likely due to a falling-out with some wanna-be actor in L.A. Or maybe she'd come home for the same reason he had…to help an ailing sibling or parent.

It got Reid to thinking about his own father, who'd taken off for parts unknown the moment his mom said "We're going to have a baby." And his mother? Well, for all her good intentions, she had a talent for choosing no-account men. The promise of a leak-proof roof and a steady supply of whiskey was enough for her. In exchange, she promised forty hours' worth of work each week…from her young son.

She had already put four ex-husbands behind her when she said "I do" to Boots Randolph. Grudgingly, Reid had to admit that Boots had taught him plenty about ranching. And while he'd been the best provider, he also had a hair-trigger temper, and Reid still bore the scars to prove it.

Had Cammi run off to California to escape a father like Boots?

The very thought made Reid clench his jaw so hard that his teeth ached, because it wouldn't take much of a blow to break someone that fragile.

No, not fragile. Cammi's demeanor—right down to that model-runway walk of hers—made it clear she was anything but delicate. He liked her "tell it like it is" way of talking, admired how she looked him dead in the eye and admitted the accident had been her fault—no excuses, no explanations.

She was agile, as evidenced by the way she'd balanced that tray of diner food on one tiny palm. Quick-witted, too, so he couldn't imagine what had distracted her enough to run that red light.

Picturing their vehicles again, gnarled and bent, made Reid cringe. It could have been worse. So much worse, as he knew all too well. Miraculously, they'd both walked away from the wreck without so much as a hangnail. "Thank God," he whispered, though even as he said it, he knew God had nothing to do with their good fortune. If the so-called Almighty had any control over things like that, Rose London wouldn't be dead, her husband wouldn't be a widower and her four daughters wouldn't have grown up without a mama.

He forced his mind away from that night. Far easier to picture Cammi, smiling, laughing, gesturing with dainty hands. Once she'd locked onto him with those mesmerizing eyes of hers, he'd been a goner. She'd looked so familiar that he'd thought at first he'd met her somewhere before. But Reid quickly dismissed the idea, because he'd never seen bigger, browner eyes. If he met a girl who looked like that, it wasn't likely he'd forget!

Reid sensed Cammi was nothing like the women who'd dogged his heels from rodeo town to rodeo town. How he could be so sure of that after spending forty-five minutes in her presence, Reid didn't know. Still, it was a good thing, in and of itself, because it had been a long time since he'd felt anything but guilt.

Guilt at being born out of wedlock. Guilt that taking care of him had made life a constant struggle for his mother. Guilt that though he'd turned himself inside-out to please his parade of stepdads, he'd never measured up. Guilt that, while rodeoing was by its nature a business for the wreckless, his devil-may-care attitude had cost him his career. And the biggest, naggin'est guilt of all…that one rainy night a decade and a half ago, he'd been behind the wheel of the pickup that killed a young wife and mother.

He tossed the covers aside, threw his legs over the edge of the bed and leaned forward, elbows balanced on knees. Head down, he closed his eyes. When he opened them, Reid stared through the French doors, deep into the quiet night. Self-pity, he believed, was one of the ugliest of human emotions. He had no business feeling sorry for himself; he'd been given a lot more than some he could name. He had his health back, for starters, a good home and a steady job, thanks to Martina and Billy. If not for this confounded disease of Billy's, he'd have the pair of them, too, for decades to come.

He'd taught himself to dwell on the positives at times like this, to get a handle on his feelings—remorse, shame, regret, whatever—because to do otherwise was like a slow, painful death. Billy and Martina needed him, and he owed it to them to get a grip.

A well-worn Bible sat on the top shelf of the bookcase across the room. Martina had put it there, years ago, when he'd come back to Amarillo for his mother's funeral. ''Whether you realize it or not,'' she'd said, ''Boots did you a favor, beating you until you'd memorized it, cover to cover.''

''How do you figure that?'' he'd griped.

She had smiled, hands folded over her flowered apron. ''Anything you need is in those pages. That's why folks call it 'The Good Book'!''

She'd been so sure of herself that Reid had almost been tempted to believe her. But blind faith had been the reason his mother had married badly…five times. If she hadn't taught him anything else, she'd shown him by example what a mind-set like that could cost a person!

Three or four steps, and he'd have Martina's Good Book in his hands. Two or three minutes, thanks to Boots's cruel and relentless lessons, and he'd locate a verse that promised solace, peace, forgiveness. A grating chuckle escaped him. *Just 'cause it's in there don't make it so,* he thought bitterly.

In all his life, he'd known just two people who were as good as their word, and both of them were fast asleep down the hall. He loved Billy and Martina more than if they'd been his flesh-and-bone parents, because they'd *chosen* to take a confused, resentful boy into their home and love him, guide him, nurture him as if he were their own. Though he'd given them plenty of reason to, they'd never thrown up their hands in exasperation.

And he wouldn't give up on them now.

Suddenly, he felt a flicker of hope. Again, Reid considered crossing the room, taking the Bible from its shelf. Maybe Martina had a point. She and Billy had made God the center of their lives for decades, and they seemed happier, more content—despite Billy's terminal illness—than anyone he'd ever known. Maybe he should at least give her advice a try.

He stood in front of the bookcase and slid the Bible halfway out from where it stood among paperback novels, Billy's comics collection and Martina's photo albums. A moment, then two, ticked silently by….

"Nah," Reid grumbled, shoving the book back

into place. He remembered, as he slid between the bedcovers, how often he'd overheard Martina's heartfelt prayers for Billy's healing.

But the healing never came. Instead, Billy's condition worsened, almost by the hour. If God could turn a deaf ear to Martina, who believed with a heart as big as her head, why would He listen to a noaccount like Reid!

Staring up at the ceiling again, he shook his head. There was no denying that Martina believed God had been the glue that held the decades-long marriage together. Once, during a visit to the Rockin' C a few years back, Reid had encountered a deep-in-prayer Martina in the living room. Glowing like a schoolgirl, she'd sung the Almighty's praises. "You talk as if He hung the moon," Reid had said, incredulous. She'd affectionately cuffed the back of his head. "He *did,* you silly goose!"

*Some*thing otherworldly was certainly responsible for their contentment and happiness. Scalp still tingling from Martina's smack, Reid had wondered if he'd live long enough to find a love like that.

"You're only twenty-seven, son. Give the Father time to lead you to the one He intends you to share your life with." As Reid opened his mouth to object, she'd added, "Think about it, you stubborn boy! If He could hang the moon, surely He can help you find your soul mate!"

Soul mate, Reid thought now. Did such a thing even exist anywhere other than in romance novels?

Romance. The word made him think of Cammi. Pretty, petite, sweet as cotton candy. When his gaze was drawn again to the gilded script on the Bible's spine, he stubbornly turned away, closed his eyes.

As he drifted off to sleep, it was Cammi's smiling face he focused on.

A few hours earlier…

"Wow, lady," the cabbie said. "This is some place you've got here."

"Isn't mine," Cammi corrected. "River Valley is my dad's."

He nodded. "Still, mighty impressive all the same."

She couldn't deny it. Anyone who'd ever seen the ranch had been impressed, if not by the three-story stone house, then by the two-lane wooden bridge leading to the circular drive, or the waterfall, hissing and gurgling beneath it. Everything had been the result of her father's design…and his own hardworking hands.

The tall double doors swung wide even before Cammi stepped out of the cab. Bright golden light spilled from the enormous foyer, painting the wraparound porch and curved flagstone walkway with a butter-yellow glow and casting her father's burly form in silhouette. A booming "Camelia, you're home!" floated to her on the damp Texas breeze. Then, his deep voice suddenly laced with concern, Lamont added, "What's with the taxi? Did you have car trouble?"

Cammi grinned at the understatement. "You could say that."

"You should've called," he said. "I'd have come for you."

Could have, should have, would have. How many times had she heard *that* before leaving home?

Lamont held out his arms and Cammi melted into them. Plenty of time to tell him about the accident—and everything else—later. For the moment, wrapped in the warmth of his embrace, she put aside the reasons she'd left home. Forgot his "you'll be sorry" speech. Forgot how determined she'd been to prove him wrong, for no reason other than that for once in her life, she'd wanted to make him proud.

Proud? So much for that! Cammi thought.

"Good to have you home, sweetie."

My, but that sounded good. Sounded right. This was where she wanted...no, where she *needed* to be. And if the length or strength of Lamont's embrace was any indicator, her father felt the same way. At least, for now. "Good to *be* home," Cammi admitted.

He released her and went for his wallet.

"Dad," she started, "I can pay the—"

But Lamont had already peeled off a fifty. "That'll cover it, right, son?" he asked, shoving the bill into the driver's hand.

"Yessir, it sure will!" Eyes wide, he waited for permission to pocket the bill.

"Keep the change," Lamont said, grabbing Cammi's bag.

The man beamed. "Sayin' 'thanks' seems lame after a tip like this!"

Grinning, Lamont saluted, then slung his arm over Cammi's shoulder. "Drive safely, m'boy," he said, guiding her toward the house. He hadn't closed the front door behind them before asking, "Where's the rest of your gear?"

"I shipped some boxes a couple of days ago. They'll be delivered tomorrow, Monday at the latest." She tugged the strap of her oversized purse, now resting firmly against his rock-hard shoulder. "Meanwhile, I have the essentials right here."

"Meanwhile," he echoed, frowning as he assessed her rain-dampened hair and still-wet clothes, "you're soaked to the skin." He nudged her closer to the wide, mahogany staircase. "Get on upstairs and take a hot shower. After you've changed into something warm and dry, meet me in the kitchen. Meantime, I'll put on a pot of decaf."

In other words, Cammi deducted, despite the late hour, he expected her to fill in the blanks—some of them, anyway—left by her long absence; she hadn't been particularly communicative by phone or letter while she'd been gone, with good reason, and she was thankful Lamont hadn't pressed her for details. Now the time had come to pay the proverbial piper. "Warm and dry sounds wonderful," she said, more because it was true than to erase the past two years from her mind.

"Everything is exactly as you left it."

How like him to keep things as they were. Though her mother had been gone thirteen years when Cammi headed west, the only things Lamont had replaced were the linens, and even those were duplicates of the originals. Something told her it was love of the purest possible kind that kept him so stubbornly attached to his beloved Rose. The fact that her dad had held on to memories about *her,* too, inspired a flood of loving warmth. "I'll just be a few minutes," Cammi said, standing on tiptoe to kiss his cheek. Almost as an afterthought, she added, "Love you, Dad."

"Love you, too."

At least for now you do, Cammi thought.

Suddenly, the prospect of being in her old room, surrounded by familiar things, rejuvenated her, and she took the steps two at a time, half listening for his oh-so-familiar warning:

"You're liable to fall flat on your face and chip a tooth, bolting up those stairs like a runaway yearling."

He'd said the same thing, dozens of times, when Cammi and her sisters were children. She stopped on the landing and smiled. "I'll be careful, Dad," she said, pressing a hand to her stomach, "I promise." He had no way of knowing she had a new and very important reason to keep that promise.

Cammi blew him a kiss and hurried to her room. The sooner she got back downstairs, the sooner she'd know if this amiable welcome was the real deal...or a temporary truce.

Real, she hoped, because she would need his emotional support these next few months, even if it might come at the price of seeing his disappointment yet again. How would she tell him that, in yet another characteristically impulsive move, she'd exchanged "I do's" with a movie stuntman in a gaudy Vegas wedding chapel? And it wouldn't just be the non-Christian ceremony he'd disapprove of.

When Reid had asked earlier if she had a husband and children, her heart had skipped a beat. For a reason she couldn't explain, it mattered what Reid thought of her. Mattered very much. So much so, in fact, that though she'd enjoyed his company, she'd rather never see him again than risk having him discover the truth about her. And if a stranger's opinion mattered that greatly, how much more difficult would it be to live with her dad's reaction!

For the past four months, since learning of Rusty's death and the baby's existence, Cammi had spent hours thinking up ways to break the news to her father. She'd hoped an idea would come to her during the long, quiet drive from California to Texas. Sadly, she still didn't have a clue how to tell him that in just five short months, his first grandchild would be born.

Lamont would be a terrific grandfather, what with his natural storytelling ability and his gentle demeanor. If only he could learn he was about to become a grandpa in the traditional way, instead of being clubbed over the head with the news.

What Cammi needed was a buffer, someone who'd distract him, temporarily, anyway, from asking questions that had no good answers. "Hey, Dad," she called from the top step, "where's Lily? I sort of expected *she'd* be the one bounding down the front walk when I got home…with some critter wrapped around her neck."

"Matter of fact, she's in the barn, nursing one of those critters right now."

Lily was the only London daughter who'd never left home. A math whiz and avid animal lover, the twenty-four-year-old more or less ran River Valley Ranch. "As much time as she spends with her animals," Cammi said, "I'll never understand how she manages to keep your ledger books straight."

"That makes two of us," Lamont said, laughing.

She ducked into her room, telling herself that if she survived coffee with her dad, she'd pay Lily and her critter a little visit. Maybe her kid sister would drop a hint or two that would help Cammi find a good way to tell them…*everything.*

A shiver snaked up her spine when she admitted there *was* no good way.

Lamont's back was to her when she rounded the corner a short while later, reminding Cammi of that night so many years ago, when she'd padded downstairs in pajamas and fuzzy slippers. "Dad," she'd whimpered, rubbing her eyes toddlerlike despite being twelve years old, "I can't sleep."

When he'd turned from the kitchen sink, his red-rimmed eyes were proof that he hadn't been able to sleep, either, that he'd been crying, too. "C'mere, sweetie," he'd said, arms extended as he settled onto the caned seat of a ladder-back chair.

She'd ignored the self-imposed rule that said a soon-to-be teenager was too old to climb into her daddy's lap, and snuggled close, cheek resting on the soft, warm flannel of his blue plaid shirt, and closed her eyes, inhaling the crisp spicy scent of his manly aftershave.

Even now, all grown up and carrying a child of her own, she remembered how safe she'd always felt when those big arms wrapped around her, how soothing it was when his thick, clumsy fingers combed through her curls. Her unborn baby deserved to feel safe and protected that way, too; had her impulsive lifestyle made that impossible? Could Lamont accept what she'd done, at least enough not to hold it against his grandchild?

It hadn't been hard to read his mind that night, the eve of Rose's funeral. What was going through his mind now? Cammi wondered. Had looking through the rain-streaked window at his long-deceased wife's autumn-yellowed hydrangeas conjured a painful memory? Had the moon, which painted a shimmering silver border around each slate-gray cloud, reminded him how much the mother of his children had always enjoyed thunderstorms?

She wouldn't tell him about Rusty and the baby tonight. Tomorrow or the next day would be more than soon enough to add to his sadness. There's a time and a place for everything, she told herself. And sensing he'd be embarrassed if she walked in and caught him woolgathering, Cammi backed up a few steps, cleared her throat and made a noisy entrance.

"Hey, Dad," she said brightly, shuffling into the kitchen on white-socked feet. "Coffee ready?"

He masked his melancholy well, she thought as he turned and smiled.

"Sure is," Lamont said. "Still drink it straight-n-plain?"

"Yessir."

"We Londons are tough, so save the milk and sugar for kindergarten kids!" they said in unison.

Laughing, father and daughter sat across from one another at the table. A moment passed, then two, before Cammi said, "So how've you been, Dad?"

"Fine, fine." He nodded, then reached across the table, blanketed her hand with his. "Question is, how're *you?*"

She looked into gray eyes that glittered with fatherly love and concern. There were a few more lines around them than she remembered, but then, worrying about her had probably put every one of them there. Cammi felt overwhelmed by guilt. He'd worked so hard to provide for his girls, all while doing his level best to be both mother and father to them. He deserved far better than what she'd always given him.

"I'd hoped to accomplish something out there—" she blurted. "Something that would make you really proud of—"

"You've always made me proud," Lamont interrupted, "just being you. You know that."

She didn't know anything of the kind, especially since her mother's accident, but it still felt good, real good, to hear him say it. Suddenly, she found herself fighting tears.

Lamont gave her hand an affectionate squeeze. "I told you before you left home that those Tinsel Town phonies didn't have enough accumulated brain matter to power a lightbulb."

He'd said that and then some!

"So how'd you expect dunderheads like that to have enough sense to see what a great li'l gal you are!" He patted her hand, then added, "I know you gave it your all, sweetie. If your best wasn't good enough for 'em, well…" He lifted his chin a notch. "Well, that's their loss."

So he thought her failure to land any decent roles in L.A. was responsible for her dour mood. Cammi was about to set the record straight when Lamont said, "You did the right thing, coming home. You have any idea what you'll do now that you're back?"

Lamont's question implied she was home to stay, and he was right. This baby growing steadily inside her deserved a stable home, deserved to be raised in a house where it would be treasured, and protected and nurtured by a big loving family. It didn't matter one whit what was good for *her*; from the moment she'd learned of its existence, Cammi had put the baby first, always, and that meant giving up her crazy ideas of stardom. She'd earned a degree in Childhood Development, had spent nearly three years teaching four- and five-year-olds before heading for L.A.

She ran a fingertip around the rim of her mug. "I made arrangements to meet with the Board of Ed first thing tomorrow. There are some openings in the Amarillo School District."

"Good plan." He slid his chair back and got to his feet. "Baked an apple pie today...."

"Baked a pie? You?" Cammi laughed. "What's this world coming to!"

"If you call following directions on the box 'baking,' then I baked a pie." He chuckled. "It was Patti's day off, see, and I got a hankering for something sweet." Unceremoniously, he plopped the dessert on the table. "Care for a slice?"

Cammi went around to his side of the table, gently shoved him back into his chair. "You tore open the package and put it in the oven, all without your housekeeper's help, I might add. Least I can do is serve it up."

She wasn't surprised, as she rummaged in the cupboards for plates, silverware and napkins, to find everything right where her mother had kept them. "More coffee?"

Lamont held out his mug, and, smiling, she topped it off.

"Did I tell you it's good to have you home?"

She folded a paper napkin and laid it beside his mug. "Yes, you did." Bending at the waist, Cammi kissed his cheek. "Did I tell you it's good to *be* home?"

Cammi didn't miss the slight hitch in his voice when he echoed her response. "Yes, you did." She slid a wedge of pie onto a plate. As he speared an apple with one tine of his fork, he added, "I sure have missed you."

She looked at him, smiling nervously, blinking. What was going on here? Her stoic, keep-your-feelings-to-yourself dad, admitting a thing like that? "Heard from Ivy or Vi lately?" she asked carefully.

"Your sisters will be here for a welcome-home celebration as soon as we can arrange it. Patti will be whipping up a special dinner for us.

Cammi had been fairly sure that, like most everything else in her life these days, her homecoming would be a fiasco. In fact, she'd been dreading the whole miserable scene so much that she'd been distracted and run the red light in Amarillo.

Memory of the accident brought Reid Alexander to mind yet again. Cammi pictured the handsome, tortured face. She knew precisely what event from her past haunted *her,* but what had painted the edgy, troubled look on his—

"So, what happened to your car?"

Cammi gave a dismissive little wave. "Little fender bender in town is all. No big deal."

Thanking God yet again that no one had been hurt,

she remembered the napkin, tucked into the front pocket of her purse, that Reid had given to her in the diner. "The mechanic will call you with an estimate," he'd said, looking as if he'd been the one responsible for the damage.

Cammi braced herself, waiting for her dad to ask whose fault the accident had been, waiting for the safety lecture that would surely follow once she admitted she'd been one hundred percent to blame.

Instead, Lamont said, "Important thing is, you're home now, safe and sound."

And so is your grandchild, she thought, thanking the Almighty again.

He shoved his empty pie plate to the center of the table. "Not bad for store-bought and frozen, eh?"

Not bad at all, Cammi thought, looking into his loving face. Not bad at all.

And pie had nothing to do with the sentiment.

As she made her way up to bed around 2:00 a.m. after having a heart-to-heart with her sister Lily in the barn, Cammi's mind drifted back to Reid. His voice and manly stance, and the bright green of his eyes set her heart to pounding, as if she were a teenage girl in the throes of a first crush.

She dreaded going to bed because she knew she wouldn't be having a peaceful night's sleep.

More than likely, she'd have nightmares induced by worries about her condition—and how Lamont would react to the same news.

Chapter Three

Reid stood beside his rumpled bed, staring at the napkin bearing Cammi's name and phone number. Thinking about her had kept him up most of the night. Shaking his head, he slapped the napkin onto the nightstand, because there didn't seem to be a single legitimate reason to call her.

Couldn't use the car repairs as an excuse, because he'd already told her the mechanic wouldn't have time to assess the damage until Monday, at the earliest. Couldn't say the tow truck driver needed information, because she already knew their vehicles had been delivered to Wilson's Garage.

What was wrong with honesty? he wondered. Why not just tell her he enjoyed her company and wanted to see her again. He could suggest a movie, or a quiet dinner, someplace where he could get to know her better.

Reid held the receiver in one hand, the napkin in the other, then noticed that his alarm clock said five-thirty. Groaning, he blew a stream of air through his teeth. What was he thinking? Not everyone got up with the cock's crow! She'd driven all the way from L.A. to Amarillo and had had a car wreck, all in one day. Surely she'd be sawing logs at this hour.

Still, he thought, palming the napkin once more, hadn't she said this was her cell phone number? More than likely, it was turned off and recharging. He could leave a message, and if she didn't return the call, he could tell himself it had somehow been lost in cyberspace....

Holding his breath, Reid punched in the digits. After three interminably long rings, her lyrical voice said, "Hi. This is Cammi."

He could almost see her, smiling, bobbing her head, big eyes flashing as she recorded the message. The mental picture distracted him so much that he didn't hear the *beep.* "Uh, hey, Cammi. It's Reid. Reid Alexander. From last night, and, uh, y'know, the accident?" He looked at his watch. "It's just past five-thirty, Saturday morning and, well, I was just wondering if..."

What if he suggested a date and she rejected him? "...if there's anything I forgot. Y'know, phone numbers, or...whatever. So, call if you need anything." He rattled off his cell phone number, even though he had seen her tuck the napkin he'd written it on into the front pocket of her purse. Reid glanced at his watch again. "I hope you're okay, 'cause, well, I've heard that sometimes a person doesn't feel the afteraffects of an accident till the next day, or even the day after that." He rubbed his face and winced. "I hear-tell aspirin is good for what ails you." *Shut up, you idiot!* he told himself. "Anyway, I hope you're all right. Thanks and—"

"You're welcome. And I'm fine. How're you?"

He felt like a colossal birdbrain, a jerk, a sappy blockheaded schoolboy. He could only hope Cammi didn't agree. "I, uh, thought I was leaving a message." No wonder he hadn't heard a *beep!*

"I got into the habit of answering the phone that way, so I'd sound in demand in case a producer ever called."

When she giggled, Reid's heart beat double time.

"I guess since I'm no longer in demand, I can start saying a simple 'hello' like everybody else, huh?"

Another merry giggle tickled his ear. He wanted to say, *First of all, you're not like everybody else.* Instead, Reid said, "You're very much in demand, at least by one beat-up cowboy."

Her tiny gasp made him grin. Would she be sitting there, wide-eyed, one hand over her mouth? he wondered.

"You're up awfully early."

"Early? Should've been up and out half an hour ago," he said, glad she hadn't hung up despite his long-winded "message" and his blatant flirtation. "But what're you doing up at this hour, if you don't mind my asking?"

Her sigh filtered through the wires, kissing his eardrum. Reid shivered involuntarily.

"No specific reason," Cammi said. "I just have… There's a lot to be done today."

Was that sadness he heard in her voice? Reid hoped not, because something told him that if anybody had earned the right to be happy, it was Cammi. "Well,

I won't keep you, then. Just wanted you to know you can call, any time, if I forgot anything.''

"You didn't forget anything, but if I remember something you might have forgotten, I'll be sure and call." After a long pause, she added, "And I hope you know you can do the same."

He nodded, then shook his head and chuckled under his breath, because of course she couldn't *see* him nodding. "Sure. Right. I'll do that." Reid cleared his throat. "Well, you take it easy, y'hear?"

"I will. You, too."

"Catch you later, then."

"Have a good one!"

If one of them didn't put a stop to this, they'd go on "ending" the conversation till sundown. Much as he'd enjoy spending the day with her, even by phone, he took the bull by the horns: "Bye, Cammi. Glad to hear you're still feeling fine."

"Thanks. Glad you're all right, too. I'll call if I hear anything from the insurance company or the mechanic."

"I'll do the same."

He put the phone back into its cradle, wondering why the room felt colder and darker.

Reid remembered that earlier, he'd pocketed Billy's note, the one with Amanda's hotel and room number. Grimacing, he fished it out. The sooner he got things cleaned up, the better. She answered on the first ring.

"Hey," he said, "I got your message and—"

"Reid, *dar*ling!" she shrieked. "How *are* you! Why haven't you *called!* I've been so *wor*ried about you!"

He sighed. "Will you be free in about an hour? I know it's early, but—"

"Oh, Reid," she cooed. "I'm *never* too busy for *you.*"

He stifled a sigh of frustration. Amanda's tendency to overemphasize even the simplest words was but one in a long list of reasons that it could never work out between them.

"When did you get into town?"

"Why, *yes*terday, of course. I called the *minute* I settled in, so we could get together and talk about *us.*"

He could tell her, here and now, that there never had been and never would be an *us,* but Reid didn't believe in taking the easy way out. The night he'd won the Silver Buckle award, Amanda had tearfully admitted she didn't have a ride home. And because Martina and Billy had drummed into his head that gentlemen treated women like ladies whether or not they deserved it, he agreed to drive her. He should have immediately put the brakes on her intense thank-you kiss in the hall outside her apartment. If he had, he wouldn't have paid for his thoughtfulness every day since.

"I didn't leave my room *once,*" Amanda was saying. "I'd just *die* if you called while I was out!"

"Mmm-hmm," he said distractedly. He had tried, over and over since that first night, to explain that one kiss doesn't seal *any* deal, least of all of the relationship kind. Her sobs had made him decide to explain things another day, when she wasn't so…emotional. *And today's that day.*

"I can hardly wait to *see* you, Reid! Did you miss me as much as I missed *you?*"

In place of a response, he said, "How 'bout I pick you up at eight, buy you some breakfa—?"

"Oh, Reid! I'd just *love* that!"

"See you at eight."

Reid felt strangely guilty after hanging up, not for severing the connection with Amanda, not for what he was about to tell her, but because it seemed this meeting with Amanda was tantamount to cheating on Cammi. He couldn't help but chuckle at that, because wouldn't it be a bitter irony if Cammi was home right now, rehearsing the same speech for him that he was about to make to Amanda!

Amusement faded fast as he imagined her, hemming and hawing as she sought a compassionate way to deliver her message. It would hurt worse than a fall from a saddle bronc, no matter what words she chose or how kindly she spoke them.

"Ridiculous," he muttered. "Face it, man…you barely know the woman!"

Still, admitting how it would sting if Cammi rejected him started a 'what goes around, comes around' mantra swirling in his head. It made him decide to set Amanda straight gently. Very gently…just in case. He half ran down the stairs, anxious to get it over with, once and for all. If he didn't waste any time, he could get the new ranch hands squared away before heading into town….

The moment he stepped into Martina's big sunny kitchen, he saw that she'd set the table. The scent of fresh-brewed coffee permeated the air, and pots and pans promising a full country breakfast were steaming on the stove.

"Good grief," he said, looking around. "What time did you get up?"

Martina handed him a glass of juice. "Never you mind. Just sit down and eat before everything gets cold."

Billy only shrugged, so Reid did as he was told; might be a lot easier for Amanda to take his "I'm not good for you" speech if he wasn't wolfing down bacon and eggs while he made it.

"I want you to have a healthy meal in your belly," Martina told her husband, "before we start out for Fort Worth."

It wasn't like Billy to comply so quickly, without so much as a teasing retort or a sly wink. Reid blamed it on nerves; Billy had never liked long drives or sleeping in hotel beds, and liked doctors' exams even less. This trip to the latest in a long list of specialists would require both.

Martina handed each man a plate piled high with link sausages, over-easy eggs, crisp golden hash browns, and buttered toast. She filled their coffee cups, then joined them at the table. Spreading homemade raspberry jam on her bread, she asked, "You okay this morning, Reid?"

He looked up, more than a little surprised at the question. Later today, she'd drive her husband all the way to Fort Worth for who-knows-what kind of prognosis. "I'm fine. How 'bout you?"

From the day Reid's mom brought him and his beat-up cardboard suitcase into this house, Martina had taken Reid under her wing, treated him like the son she'd never had. He couldn't love her more if she were his mother. A guilty thought rapped at the edges of his mind: Reid did love her more than his own mother. But then, Martina had *earned* that love.

"Never mind about me."

"I'm fine," he said again.

Her left brow rose, the way it always did when she thought he was holding something back. "You're not all stiff and sore? After that collision last night?"

He reached past the Eiffel Tower saltshaker and the Big Ben pepper mill to grab her hand. "Nope."

She still didn't believe him, and the proof was that in addition to raising her brow, Martina had tucked in one corner of her mouth.

God knows the poor woman had enough on her slender shoulders, what with all she did around the house and helping Billy with Rockin' C business. And now this mind-numbing death sentence.... "Honest," he added in a voice much too bright for his mood, "I'm right as rain. Fit as a fiddle. Sound as a dollar."

Billy chuckled as Martina sighed and shook her head. "Well, all right. If you say so. But there's a bottle of aspirin in the medicine cabinet, just in case."

Reid couldn't help but smile around a bite of spicy sausage, because truth was, his neck did feel a speck creaky, and a cramp in his lower back had nagged at him several times during the night. He blamed the long, sleepless hours for his minor discomforts; seemed every time he closed his eyes, he saw Cammi, smiling that *smile* of hers…brown eyes flashing, dimple deepening, musical voice reminding him of the wind chimes outside Martina's kitchen window. How was a man supposed to get any shut-eye when—

"What in thunder did you put in those sausages?" Billy asked his wife.

Her brow furrowed.

He used his butter knife as a pointer. "You can see for yourself the boy's off in la-la land."

Reid stopped chewing and smiled nervously under their scrutiny. He looked from Martina to Billy and back again. "What?"

The couple exchanged a knowing glance, and Martina giggled.

He put down his fork. "C'mon guys. Cut it out. You're gonna give me a complex."

"This girl who ran into you," Martina began, "is she pretty?"

Reid felt his cheeks flush. Because Billy and Martina were on to him? Or because Martina's question gave him yet another mental picture of Cammi? "She's okay," he said, though *pretty* didn't begin to describe her.

"What's her name?" Martina asked.

"Cammi Carlisle."

"Carlisle," Billy said out loud. "Don't know the name."

"Must be new in town," his wife told him.

Reid helped himself to another sausage. "She was on her way home from spending a couple years in California when we, uh, met. Said she'd lived here all her life before that."

Billy and Martina looked puzzled.

"Maybe Carlisle is her married name. Maybe her parents are divorced and—"

Reid didn't hear Billy's explanation, because his mind had locked on the word *married*. Unconsciously, his fingers tightened around his fork handle. Heart thundering as his ears grew hot, he remembered asking Cammi if her husband's job had taken her away from Amarillo. The only word he could come up with to describe how she'd looked was *sad*. Even now, he heard the sorrowful note in her voice when she'd answered. Her reaction conjured more questions than answers.

Maybe Cammi had followed some guy to California. Maybe they'd tied the knot while they were out there, and things went sour, so she'd come home to put an end to it. That sure would explain why her mind hadn't been on the road when she ran the red light.

Then again, maybe there hadn't been a husband at all, and she'd come home for no reason other than that she couldn't cut it in Hollywood.

The real question was, what did he care?

At that moment, all Reid wanted was to get off by himself. It would take half an hour to drive to Amanda's hotel. He'd have plenty of time to roll those notions around in his head a time or two on the way over, see if he could figure out why the idea of a man in Cammi's life nagged at him like the aftereffects of a bug bite.

Reid scooted his chair back and got to his feet. "Great meal, Martina, as usual." He carried his plate and silverware to the sink, grabbed his jean jacket from the wall peg and opened the back door.

He was half in, half out when she said, "Where are you going in such an all-fired hurry?"

"Got those new guys starting work today, remember. Don't want them lollygaggin', 'specially not on their first day." He nodded toward the outbuildings. "Might as well put them right to work on that fence."

Billy was leaning back in his chair, preparing to agree, when Martina said, "Before you go, I have a favor to ask you."

Reid stepped back into the kitchen. "I'll do it."

Her brows rose. "But you don't even know what it is yet!"

"Can't think of anything I'd refuse you."

She smiled, then folded her hands in front of her. "Well, you know how terrible I am with directions." She bit her lower lip, glancing quickly at her husband before meeting Reid's eyes. "And you know Billy can't drive anymore, so I was wonder—"

"Say no more," he interrupted. "What time were the two of you planning to hit the road?"

"Right after lunch," Billy said.

Reid put his hands in his pockets and nodded. More than enough time to get this nasty business with Amanda *and* the new ranch hands taken care of. "I'll just get the boys started, make sure they have enough to keep them occupied till we get back. I have a, uh, errand in town, but I'll be back by noon. We can head out whenever you're ready."

Martina gave a relieved sigh. "I had a feeling we could count on you." She brightened to add, "I took the liberty of booking a room for you at our hotel."

The long drive before and after the doctor's appointment would wear Billy to a frazzle, so despite the fact that he hated hotels, Reid would stay the night.

"All I can say," Billy put in, "is *this* doc better be worth the trip." He gave Martina a stern yet loving look. "Those last four quacks weren't worth their weight in feathers. You've run me all over, looking for a—"

"A miracle. Yes, that's right," she finished for him. Tears filled her dark eyes. Suddenly, she gripped her husband's hand, gave it a little shake. "I have faith, mister, and I won't rest until we've exhausted every possible option!"

On his feet now, Billy gathered her close and nuzzled her neck. "Aw, now, honeypot, don't get all weepy on me." He pressed an affectionate kiss to her cheek. "Don't pay me any mind. Y'know I love you to pieces for all you're doin' to save my ornery hide, right?"

Eyes closed, Martina nodded and pressed her freshly kissed cheek against his knuckles. If Reid hadn't already known how absolutely devoted she was to Billy, this scene would have made it obvious.

Her wavering breath pulsed in the quiet room.

So as not to disturb them, Reid slipped out the door, feeling like an interloper for eavesdropping on this very private, very loving moment.

Something nagged at the periphery of his consciousness:

He'd never been one to envy what others had…but it sure would be nice to know a love like that before he met his Maker.

After giving the ranch hands their orders, Reid drove to Amanda's hotel and found her waiting for him outside the entrance. "I *figured* you'd be driving some kind of monster truck,'' she said, giggling when she opened the passenger door, "so I wore *blue* jeans.''

She sidled up, intent on planting a kiss right on his lips. He gave her his cheek instead, and pretended not to notice the disappointment that registered on her face. She recovered quickly, though—he had to give her that. After a second or two of silence, she snuggled close.

"I hate to sound like an old codger," he began, pointing at the passenger seat, "but you need to slide right back over there and buckle your seat belt." He stared straight ahead. If Rose London had been wearing her seat belt thirteen years ago, she might have survived the accident. Since that night, he'd been a stickler when it came road safety.

But Amanda had no way of knowing that, and her wide-eyed expression proved it. "Had a fender bender last night," he added, "so it's making me more cautious than usual."

"How sweet," was her breathy reply.

Amanda chattered about turbulence during her flight as Reid drove to Georgia's Diner and parked in the lot, babbled about too few towels in her hotel room as they walked inside, yammered about Amarillo's gray skies and chilly temperatures as they scanned menus. "You look *won*derful," she said, once the gum-snapping waitress had left with their order.

Reid knew she expected him to return the compliment, but to say anything flattering right now would only make his speech that much harder to deliver. *No point putting off till tomorrow what you can do today,* he silently quoted Billy. Taking a deep breath, he plunged in, saying it was all his fault that she'd come to believe they had a future as anything but friends. To spare her feelings, he called himself a fool, a self-centered jerk, a boor.

To his amazement, Amanda didn't resort to tears, didn't disagree. In fact, she said nothing, nothing at all. Instead, she simply stood and gathered her things before walking woodenly out the door. Groaning inwardly, Reid put a twenty on the table to cover the cost of the food they'd ordered, and followed her. He caught up to her on the entrance to the parking lot.

"Amanda," he began, "don't go away mad. There's no need—"

She threw herself into his arms and held on tight. Reid looked up, as if the answer to this problem was written on the underside of a rain cloud. He was about to offer to drive her back to the hotel when movement across the street caught his eye.

Cammi—in tiny black shoes and a bright white sweater—mouth agape and eyes wide, looking directly at him.

It was as if the world had come to a dead halt. Cammi no longer heard the steady din of traffic, didn't see sparrows flitting to and fro, pecking the sidewalk in search of food scraps dropped by hurrying pedestrians, couldn't feel the biting blast of autumn wind against her cheeks. She wasn't even feeling the rush of satisfaction from the successful interview she'd just come from with the principal of Puttman Elementary that had resulted in a teaching position.

Instead, she was aware only of Reid, locked in an intimate embrace with a tall, striking blonde.

It made no sense why jealousy reared its ugly head, started her heart beating faster.

Reid hadn't mentioned a woman last night in Georgia's Diner. But then, why would he? He certainly didn't owe her any explanations. The sight of him, face half buried in the blonde's long, gleaming tresses, made her fumble-footed, and she tripped over a protruding blob of hard tar, squeezed into a crack in the curb.

Tires skidded, horns honked, brakes squealed as she landed on hands and knees in the road. She felt ridiculous, crawling around in a small circle, grabbing up the tube of lipstick and ballpoint pens that had spilled from her purse.

She had no idea when Reid had crossed the street, or when he'd knelt beside her. But there he was, lips a fraction of an inch from hers, smiling as she stuffed a rat-tail comb, a pack of tissues and a quarter into her bag.

"We've gotta quit meetin' this way," he drawled. Cammi giggled nervously, despite the dull ache in her lower back, despite the burning, bloody scrapes on her knees and the palms of her hands.

As they neared the curb, a wave of nausea and dizziness staggered her. But, just as he had the night before, Reid steadied her.

"You okay?" he asked, voice laced with concern.

She was about to answer, when the blonde he'd been hugging so tightly flounced up. "Well," she huffed, "at least *now* I understand why you wanted to *end* things." She blinked mascara-blackened lashes at Cammi. "I hope you'll be *very* happy, following your rodeo *cowboy* from town to town." Glaring at Reid through narrowed eyes, she added, "I feel it only fair to warn you, you *won't* be the only one!" With that, she spun on her stiletto heels and click-clacked off. "And don't you even *think* about following me, Reid Alexander," she tossed over her shoulder.

Reid seemed torn between helping Cammi and fixing things with the angry woman. "I'm okay," Cammi assured him. "Really. Now hurry, or she'll get—"

He met Cammi's eyes. "Trust me, Amanda is fine. She's like a cat…always lands on her feet." Then his eyebrows knitted with worry. "Wish I could say the same for you," he added, inspecting her scraped palms. He led her to the bus stop bench and sat her down. "Here, let's have a look at you, see if anything else is bleeding or—"

"I'm fine, honest." She nodded toward the blonde. "But she isn't. You'd better go after her, before—"

Reid tugged a neatly pressed blue bandanna from his back pocket and gently brushed road grit from her hands. "You've done a pretty good job of scratching yourself up."

But Cammi barely heard him as she watched Amanda step into a taxi and slam the door, hard. "Oh, wow. Oh man. Just look what I've gone and done this time." Hanging her head, she sighed. "I'm so sorry," she stammered. "If I wasn't such a clumsy oaf—"

"Now, cut that out," he ordered. "You don't have a thing to be sorry for."

Cammi studied his handsome, caring face. She'd

never seen that much concern on Rusty's face, not in all the months she'd known him. She pointed to the cab. "She's leaving, and—"

"You can't end what never began."

"Maybe I hit my head when I fell," she said, rubbing her temples, "and addled my brains even more than usual, because that makes no sense whatsoever."

Chuckling, Reid slid an arm around her waist and pulled her to her feet. "Let me buy you a cup of coffee, and I'll explain." He paused. "You were headed for Georgia's, right?"

She nodded. "Yes. I was in town interviewing for a teaching position at Puttman Elementary and thought I'd go into Georgia's for a cup of tea."

"How did the interview go?"

"I got the job." She smiled. "I'll be teaching fourth graders."

"Congratulations!" Reid said. "How about I keep you company at Georgia's, but what-say we cross with the traffic light this time."

"Okay, but it's not nearly as adventurous...."

She liked the sound of his laugh and wished there was a way she could hear a lot more of it. But in her condition…

Reid chose the same table they'd shared last night, ordered coffee for himself and asked the waitress to bring Cammi a cup of herbal tea. "Something to soothe your nerves," he explained when the girl left. "You might want to make an appointment with an eye doctor."

"Eye doctor?"

"You had a dizzy spell last night, too, as I recall."

He shook his head. "Maybe you need glasses or something."

Cammi took a deep breath, let it out slowly. Might as well just get it out in the open, she thought. "I don't need glasses, Reid. I need a bassinet."

Reid grinned, then snickered, then frowned. "A...a *what?*"

"Uh-huh. You heard right. A bassinet." She nodded as she saw understanding dawn on his face. "I'm four months pregnant."

His gaze went immediately to the third finger of her left hand, where the thin gold wedding band gleamed in the fluorescent light. "But...but—" He licked his lips. "But I thought... You said... You told me you weren't married," he stammered.

"My husband died four months ago. In an accident." No point spilling *all* the beans, Cammi thought, remembering the shame of hearing who Rusty's passenger had been. She'd save the "how" and "with whom" for a later conversation. If there *was* a later conversation.

Reid grabbed her hands and leaned forward. "Good grief, Cammi, why didn't you tell me about this last night?" He slapped one hand over his eyes. "I feel like a monster, bellowing at you the way I did." When he came out of hiding, he said softly, "I'm sorry."

Shaking her head, Cammi retrieved her hands, tucked them into her lap. "Nothing for you to be sorry about. I—"

"I kept asking myself," he interrupted, "what could distract a smart woman like you enough to run a red light." Reid ran a hand through his hair. "A widow just four months, and having a…" He blinked. "Having a baby, yet. I'm such a heel!"

She abruptly changed the subject.

"So who was the blonde?" she asked.

"Started following me around the rodeo circuit a couple years ago. I tried to tell her I wasn't what she was looking for, but—"

"Reid Alexander?" she blurted. "You're *that* Reid Alexander! Now I know why your name sounded so familiar. Wow. Can I have your autograph? You've probably earned more buckles than any cowboy in the history of the rodeo!"

When he blushed, Cammi's heart skipped a beat. "Tell me all about it," she said, sipping her tea.

She loved the deep, gravelly sound of his voice, the way his left brow rose now and then, and the way only one side of his mouth turned up with each grin. His green eyes flashed when he talked about the competitions, darkened when he spoke of the shoulder injury that ended his career, dulled when he told her about his friend Billy's terminal illness.

"We're heading to Fort Worth later today," he said in conclusion, "to see if this specialist has a miracle cure."

"I'll pray for him," Cammi said. "And for a safe trip there and back, too."

She didn't understand why, but suddenly he seemed angry. Had she said something wrong?

Suddenly, pain like none she'd experienced sliced through her midsection. Biting her lower lip, she grimaced.

He was on his feet and beside her in a heartbeat. "What's the matter?"

Try as she might, Cammi couldn't find her voice. Squinting her eyes shut, she gripped her stomach and prayed, *Not the baby, Lord. Please don't let it be the baby.*

Reid slid into the booth beside her, draped an arm over her shoulders. "Is there anything I can do to hel—" He leaned back, eyes focused on the red vinyl seat. "Cammi," he said slowly, deliberately, quietly, "you're…you're bleeding."

Cammi looked down as tears filled her eyes. "Oh, no," she whispered, "no…."

"Georgia," Reid bellowed, scooping Cammi up in his powerful arms, "call the emergency room. Tell them we're on the way!"

Ordinarily, the feisty older woman would have balked at being ordered about that way. But one look at Cammi, and Georgia nodded. "You bet," she said, grabbing the phone.

"By the time an ambulance could get here," he told Cammi, backing out the door, "we'll be halfway to the hospital."

Somehow, he managed to get the pickup truck's passenger door opened with one hand, then gently deposited her inside. "Don't look so scared, pretty lady," he said, buckling her seat belt, "everything will be all right."

Leaning against the headrest, she closed her eyes. *Stay calm,* she told herself. *Steady breaths, take it easy…because the Father is with you….*

Reid turned on the headlights and the hazard lights and put the truck in gear. "It'll be all right," he said again as the tires squealed onto the road.

"I hope so," she admitted. But already, she'd bled

another puddle on the truck's bench seat. ''Miscarriage,'' she sighed.

Reid reached across the seat to squeeze her hand. ''Keep a good thought, okay?''

Tears streamed down her cheeks. ''Pray, Reid,'' she managed to say. ''Please, pray for me...''

Chapter Four

If he thought for a minute it would do a lick of good, Reid would ask the Good Lord to halt all the other traffic between here and the hospital. Would ask to be delivered directly to the emergency room.

The childish wish quickly faded when he took a look at Cammi and saw her lovely face contorted with pain and fear. He couldn't even put his arms around her, hold her close and promise to stave off anything and everything that might harm her...not if he wanted to get her safely to the E.R. as fast as humanly possible.

Reid patted her hand, feeling like an idiot each time he repeated "Don't worry" and "It'll be all right." She needed solid support, not empty assurances. If he had the power, he'd move heaven and earth to spare her this torment.

Anger made him squeeze the steering wheel tighter. *He* didn't have that kind of power, but *God* did. Didn't the Good Book say "Ask and ye shall receive''? Cammi had asked, no, *pleaded* was more like it, for Him to spare her baby. Yet, as the seconds turned into minutes and the minutes steadily mounted, she grew paler and weaker…and still her precious Lord hadn't acted.

Barely half an hour had passed since she'd sat across from him in Georgia's Diner, sipping tea and calmly telling him how four months ago, in the space of a few hours, she'd become a widow and learned about the baby. He didn't think it strange that she'd glossed over the particulars of the accident that killed her husband; Reid had never been the type to dwell on the gory details, either. But she'd been downright happy to talk about the baby. "This kid changed my whole life for the better," she'd said, joy in her voice and glittering from her dancing brown eyes. "I can hardly wait to meet him…or her!"

Though Cammi had hardly made a sound since they'd left the diner, he knew she was in pain—physical and emotional. Rather than cry out, instead of whimpering, she sat quietly, alternately holding her breath and panting—something else they had in common: he'd handled the broken bones, muscle pulls and torn ligaments in exactly the same way. Reid didn't think for a minute that she'd adopted her stoic demeanor just for his benefit. Her behavior last night—taking full blame for the accident—told him she was made of sturdy stuff, the "no point cryin'" over spilt milk," "grin and bear it" type. Just one more reason to respect and admire her.

"It'll be all right," he said yet again, wishing he could turn back the clock to a time when she had reason to grin.

Last time he'd spoken those words, Cammi had whispered, "I hope so." She obviously hadn't intended him to hear her greatest fear, whispered on the heels of what appeared to be another severe cramp: "Miscarriage…" Much as he hated to admit it, he thought so, too.

Seemed unfair, comparing a li'l gal as gorgeous as Cammi to a pregnant mare, but it was the only parallel he could draw from. He'd spent years around the stables, and knew the signs when he saw them: Cammi was losing her baby, if she hadn't already. He'd succeeded in saving a few foals in his day…and had failed a time or two as well. It had been hard, mighty hard, watching the mamas nuzzle limp, leggy newborns, determined to bring them 'round with soft, loving snorts and whispery whinnies. He'd risked being stomped more times than he could count, going into the stalls to carry the lifeless critters away. But the "out of sight, out of mind" theory, he'd learned, didn't heal the hurtin' any quicker in the four-legged world than in the two-legged kind.

Most times, thankfully, after a few rough days of searching for their young'uns, the fillies came to grips with the cold, cruel facts. But sometimes, the heartbroken mothers were never the same again. Cammi seemed strong enough to survive her loss, but then, every mare that gave up after the death of a foal had surprised him….

Cammi's raspy, trembling voice broke into his thoughts. "Reid. Please…pray for me?"

Pray? he thought. To the God who had let her husband die, who had let *this* happen to her—all in the space of a couple of months? Reid couldn't believe his ears. He blamed her blood loss, delirium, panic…what else could make her spout such gibberish?

He chanced a peek at her, at the tears glistening on her long dark lashes, at the hope emanating from her big frightened eyes, and realized she'd meant it, right down to the last syllable. Foolish as it seemed, Reid couldn't refuse her anything, especially at a time like this. If prayer would bring Cammi even one moment's comfort…

Reid cleared his throat, tried to remember something—anything—Martina had taught him, tried to conjure any of the hundreds of passages he'd memorized under his stepfather's brutal hand. Isaiah 49: 13 seemed as good as any: '"Sing, O heavens; and be joyful, O earth; and break forth into singing, O mountains,"' he recited, '"for the Lord hath comforted his people, and will have mercy upon his afflicted."'

Eyes closed, Cammi heaved a shaky sigh as Reid continued with Revelation 7:17. '"For the Lamb which is in the midst of the throne shall feed them, and shall lead them unto living fountains of waters: and God shall wipe away all tears from their eyes."'

He saw her slowly nod as a peaceful smile kissed the corners of her mouth. "Perfect," she said softly. "And now, will you pray?"

The breath caught in his throat. If chapter and verse wasn't praying, what was?

But even as he asked the question, Reid knew that what Cammi wanted, what she needed from him now: A heartfelt, plainspoken plea, not for herself, but for her baby.

He felt like a hypocrite for giving so much as half a thought to the idea of asking *God* for help. A lifetime of unanswered prayers and bitter disappointments had taught him that the Lord, if He even existed, had turned His turn back on Reid, on Martina and Billy, on so many good people Reid had known.

Still, the Bible verses had definitely calmed her, as evidenced by her now regular, shallow breaths. He'd heard enough from-the-heart-pleas in his stepfather's fire-and-brimstone church to know how it should be done. Wouldn't help, he thought again, but what could it hurt?

"Lord," he began, "You taught us that with faith, nothing is impossible, so bless Your daughter, Cammi, now." She'd need strength of the superhuman kind, Reid acknowledged silently, to accept what the E.R. doctors would say about her pregnancy. "She believes You'll help her, believes You'll keep her baby safe and sound, right up to the moment You've chosen to bring it into this world."

It was hard to continue, because when she squeezed his hand, a tiny sob issued from her, causing a hard lump to form in his throat. Oh, what he wouldn't do to keep her safe and sound! "And Lord," he added, "keep *Cammi* safe and sound. We ask these things in Your name…."

Together, they uttered a quiet "Amen."

One second, then two, ticked silently by before she said, "Thank you, Reid," and nodded off.

Dread wrapped around him like a cold wet wind. "Only a few more minutes," he said, squeezing her small hand. "I can see the E.R. entrance sign."

It reminded him of the last time he'd been to this

hospital, when he'd visited his mother. She lay pale and gaunt against flowery bedsheets provided by the nice hospice ladies. He'd barely stuck a boot tip into her room when she ordered him to leave, to stay away until after she'd gone to meet her Maker. "I don't want you to remember me this way," she'd whimpered, turning her face to the wall. Fiery rage had burned inside him, because he'd childishly—foolishly—expected medical science to do what God had refused to do. Despite the torturous treatments they'd put her through, the cancer continued to grow, until one day, mercifully, she slipped into a coma.

That's when he went back to the rodeo, and he didn't return again until Martina called to say Billy had arranged everything—the wake, the funeral, the headstone. Reid was alone at his mother's grave when he swore the next time he set foot in a hospital, it would be feetfirst—with a tag wrapped around his big toe.

Unfortunately, he'd seen the inside of too many hospitals across the country. The risks he took riding savage, untamed beasts told the rodeo world that Reid Alexander, "All-Around Cowboy," had no fear. In truth, he flat-out didn't give a hoot what happened to him. How ironic, he thought, that having nothing to live for had made him a star.

At the moment, though, Reid cared very much, because this small, helpless woman beside him *needed* him to care. He stomped the truck's brakes outside the E.R.'s double-wide entry, leaped from the cab without bothering to close the driver's side door, and bolted into the hospital. "I've got a woman out there," he bellowed, pointing frantically, "and she's had a miscarriage. She's bleeding badly, and—"

The nearest nurse looked up from her clipboard, peered over black half glasses at his shirt and blue jeans. He followed her gaze. Until that moment, Reid hadn't realized how much of Cammi's blood had soaked into his own clothes.

"Bring her inside and take a seat," the nurse droned, pointing at two empty chairs in the waiting room.

Eyes narrowed and lips thinned by fear and frustration, he took a step closer, thumped a forefinger on the form she'd been filling out. "Sprained ankles and upset stomachs can wait," he growled. With each word, his voice escalated in volume and vehemence. "but the lady outside *can't*."

She must have heard hundreds of similar speeches. Shrugging, she went back to her scribbling. "Like I said, take a seat and we'll get to you when we—"

Reid spotted a gurney behind her and, stomping toward it, he snarled, "When I get back in here, there had better be a doctor standing where you are." He didn't wait for her to protest, didn't tell her what he'd do if his order wasn't carried out. Instead, Reid blasted the wheeled cot through the doors and parked it alongside Billy's pickup.

One look at Cammi, slumped against the window, was enough to turn his red-hot rage into ice-blue fear. She'd been pale as a ghost when he'd left her mere moments ago; in the short time he'd been inside, she'd gone whiter still.

"Cammi, honey," he said softly, "we're goin' inside now, okay?" He eased his arms under her, tenderly lifted her from the passenger seat and lay her on the gurney. Reid draped his jean jacket over her, then hurried toward the E.R. entrance, taking care to avoid cracks in the sidewalk that might jar her.

"Hey, buddy," an orderly said, "you can't leave your truck there. We need that space for the ambulances when—"

He tossed the man his keys. "Be my guest," he snapped. "I'm kinda busy right now."

"Easy, Reid…" Cammi whispered.

Was he hearing things?

"…unless you want the E.R. docs to admit you, too, after you've had a stroke—or someone punches your lights out."

That she'd be concerned about *him* at a time like this said a mouthful about the kind of human being she was. From the instant their eyes met last night, he'd felt compelled to protect her from anything and everything that could harm her. What she'd said just now made him want that even more.

He was about to say something comforting, something consoling, when he spotted a man in a white lab coat. "Doc!" he shouted. "Hey, Doc!"

Brows raised, the fellow pointed to himself.

"Yeah, you," Reid hollered, pushing the gurney toward him. "This li'l gal is having a miscarriage. She's lost a lot of blood and—"

One look was all it took. Immediately, the doctor took control, barking orders to nurses and aides as he steered the gurney through the "Staff Only" doors to the emergency room. "Did you see the gal with the clipboard?"

Reid ran alongside him. "Nurse Ratchet, y'mean?"

The doctor grinned slightly. "Tell her I said you're to provide whatever info she needs on this patient."

Cammi could barely keep her eyes open. Who would defend her if he wasn't with her?

"Do it *now*," he insisted. "Name's Lucas. Brandon Lucas."

Reid grasped Cammi's hand, brought it to his lips. "I'll be right back, promise."

She nodded weakly, and in a barely audible voice said, "I know. I'll be fine...."

"'Course you will." She *had* to be, because—

"The nurse?" Lucas reminded him, then snapped shut the curtains surrounding Cammi's cubicle.

Reid stood there a second, unable to decide whether to burst in, or to do what the doctor ordered.

"Sooner you get it done, buddy," Lucas said through the pastel-striped material, "the sooner you can come back and hold her hand."

He pictured her, weak and alone, small and vulnerable, and realized there was no place on earth he'd rather be. But Lucas was right—the sooner he provided that nurse with whatever facts might help in treating Cammi, the sooner he'd be with her, making sure no one overlooked a single detail.

Lord, he prayed as he ran to the waiting room, *watch over her.*

Cammi hadn't so much as moaned through the tests and procedures. Watching the way she endured it all reminded him of the wild filly Billy had brought home from auction a decade or so ago—uncomplaining, no matter what paces they put her through. It made him chuckle to himself, realizing that twice, now, he'd compared Cammi to a horse. Ridiculous for a lot of reasons, starting with how petite she was.

He sat beside her as he had in the E.R., as he had while they prepped her for surgery, as he had in post-op…right arm resting on her hospital bed, fingers linked with hers. Now and then, when she shifted, the dim overhead night-light glinted from her wedding band. It was a cold, hard reminder of her connection to another life, another love. He knew, even as jealousy surged inside him, that he had no reason—no right—to feel this way. *You barely know the woman,* he reminded himself.

But that wasn't true. For a reason he couldn't explain, Reid felt as if he'd known Cammi all his life, as if some higher power had deliberately caused their paths to cross.

Better, smarter, safer, he decided, to focus on the small stuff, like the fact that she rested more peacefully when he wrapped his hand around hers.

Reid ignored the ache in his shoulder, already weakened by the punishing fall he'd taken from Ruthless, that monstrous-mean Brahman. He concentrated on how he'd rolled from the bull's sharp hooves just in time to keep from being trampled, instead of remembering that Ruthless had ended his rodeo career. The discomfort of sitting in this position was secondary to what Cammi needed. Besides, she'd survived so much in these past few months that it made Reid feel good, being the one to provide this small solace for her now.

Almost as though she'd read his mind, Cammi turned toward him, her face less wan now, her eyes a bit brighter. "You don't have to stay, Reid. I'm fine. Honest."

He shook his head, gave her hand a slight squeeze. No way he'd leave. For one thing, she would need someone with her when the surgeon came in to tell her about the baby. "Until your dad or one of your sisters takes my place, I'm stayin' put." With his free hand, he tucked a dark curl behind her ear. "Who do you want me to call first?"

She gasped quietly and covered her mouth with the fingertips of one hand.

"What? Are you in pain? Want me to get a doctor in here?"

"No—at least, not the physical kind."

He didn't understand, and said so.

"Your clothes. Look what I've done to your clothes! I've ruined them."

Only then did he remember the deep maroon stains covering his entire midsection. "Work duds," he said, sloughing it off. "Don't give it another thought." He didn't like the tiny worry furrow that had formed on her brow. In an attempt to erase it, he said, "So, who can I call for you?"

Cammi stared at the ceiling and bit her lower lip. "My dad," she said after a while, "I suppose."

She reminded him of someone, but for the life of him, Reid couldn't think who. He was far more interested in why she sounded so apprehensive at the mention of her father. He tried again to change the subject, flipping open his cell phone and doing his best to imitate a nasal-voiced operator. "May I have your number please…."

Grinning, Cammi recited it while Reid dialed.

"Don't give him too many details," she said. Almost as an afterthought, she added, "No point making him worry."

Nodding, Reid counted the rings.

"Lamont London," answered a deep, gravelly voice.

London? *Now* he knew why Cammi looked so familiar: She was the spitting image of Rose London—the woman he'd hit with his pickup...the woman who'd died that rainy night so many years ago! Reid swallowed, hard. Maybe he'd be lucky and there were two Lamont Londons in Amarillo, because if *this* one was—

"I don't have all day," the man griped. "Who is this?"

He'd recognize that angry Texas drawl in a shoulder-to-shoulder crowd at New York's Penn Station. And why wouldn't he, when he'd been hearing it in his nightmares for years. "I, uh, I'm calling about your daughter, sir," he said. "Cammi wants you to know she's fine, but she needs you to—"

"Cammi? Where is she? And if she's fine, why can't she talk to me herself?" Lamont demanded.

Reid could almost picture him, big and broad as a grizzly and every bit as threatening. "She's kinda groggy right now."

"Groggy?" Concern hardened his tone even more. "Groggy from what? Confound it, boy, I want some answers, and I want 'em *now!*"

"Then, you'd best get yourself over here and talk to her doctor." Reid told Lamont the name of the hospital, rattled off Cammi's room number and snapped the phone shut. He felt a mite guilty, ending

the conversation so abruptly. After what Lamont had
gone through on the night of his wife's death, being
summoned to a hospital this way would surely
awaken bad memories.

It awakened a few haunting memories for Reid,
too, and the hairs on the back of his neck stood at
attention as he remembered that night—Lamont's
menacing glare, the hostile accusations he'd hurled
outside the O.R.

Even at fourteen, Reid understood why Lamont
blamed him for the accident that had clearly been
Rose's fault. Grief and sorrow had stolen the man's
ability to reason things out, erased rational thought
from his mind. Years later, Reid understood it all even
better. If *he* had spent years sharing life, love and
children with the girl of his dreams, and a pickup-
driving boy had ended it all, well, in Lamont's boots,
Reid would have been a hundred times harder on that
knock-kneed young'un!

Images of the scene shook him more than he cared
to admit. But Cammi needed his calm reassurances
now, so he shoved the black thoughts to the back of
his mind. He pocketed the phone.

"I expect your dad will be here in…" He searched
for a phrase, something that would convince Cammi
her father would soon be here for her. Martina was
fond of saying "quick as a bunny," so he tried it on
for size. The moment the silly, feminine-sounding
words were out of his mouth, Reid cringed.

It was so good to see her smile that he couldn't
help mirroring her expression. "What're you grinning
about?"

"You're a very sweet man, Reid Alexander."

Sweet? He'd been called a lot of things in his day, but "sweet" wasn't one of them.

"Because something tells me 'quick as a bunny' isn't part of your usual cowboy vocabulary." She paused to lick her dry lips, then added a sleepy "So, thanks."

Thanks? For what? he wondered, holding a straw to her mouth. "Slow an' easy, now," he said as she sipped. After returning the mint-green cup to the night table, he finger-combed dark bangs from her forehead. "What-say you close your eyes, try and catch a few winks before your dad gets here."

She tilted her head, making him want to gather her close, hold her so long and so tight that nothing could ever get close enough to hurt her again.

"Thanks," she repeated.

This time he asked his question aloud. "Thanks for what?"

"Oh, just..." Cammi shrugged. "I don't know what I would have done if you hadn't been there for me today, that's what."

Her voice still hadn't regained its lyrical quality and her lower lip trembled when she spoke, he noticed. Had she overheard the doctors and nurses discussing her case? Did she already know she'd lost the baby, or merely sense it?

"I have a lot of explaining to do once my dad gets here," she said on the heels of a ragged sigh.

He continued stroking her hair, amazed by its silky texture, trying to count the many shades of brown that gleamed among the satiny tresses. "Explaining?"

Another sigh. "I never got around to telling him

about the wedding, so he has no idea I was married, let alone that I'm a widow.''

Reid wondered why Cammi had eloped, especially considering it was common knowledge that long ago, Lamont had earned his title as one of the wealthiest men in Texas. He couldn't help feeling sorry for the big guy, because not even all his money could buy him out of hearing about the secret wedding, the death of a son-in-law he'd never met, the loss of a grandchild he knew nothing about—all in one fell swoop.

She met his eyes. ''Uh-huh. I see by the shocked look on your face that you're beginning to get the picture.''

Having been on the receiving end of Lamont's wrath, he saw far more than she realized. Reid frowned. ''You're safe. What else could matter to the man?''

As if she hadn't heard him, Cammi said, ''He'll be so disappointed in me.'' Tears formed in the corners of her dark eyes. ''Not that he isn't used to that after all these years of being my father. Just once, I'd like to do something right…something he'd be proud of!''

Reid lifted her hand to his lips and gently kissed each slender finger. ''You're safe and sound,'' he said again, more forcefully this time. ''He loves you, I'm sure, so that's all he's gonna care about.''

''From your lips to God's ear.''

He bit back the urge to say, *What's God got to do with it?* If the Almighty had been doing His job up there, Reid thought, Cammi wouldn't be lying here now, worrying how her father would take the news. ''Get some sleep,'' he said instead. ''You're lookin' a mite pasty-faced.''

"My, but you're good for a girl's ego."

Smiling, Reid used the palm of his hand to gently close her eyes. "Shh," he whispered, kissing her forehead. He hadn't noticed till now all the faint freckles that dotted the bridge of her nose. "Say another word and I'll be forced to take drastic measures."

Her delicately arched brows rose slightly.

"I'll have to sing you to sleep," he explained, "and believe me, my lullabies sound scarier'n a coyote's howl."

"Oh, I don't know," she whispered. "After all you've done for me today, anything that comes out of your handsome mouth will be music to my years." Cammi sighed. "I'll go to sleep, but only to spare the ears of the patients down the hall, mind you."

Cammi was fast asleep before Reid finished tucking the covers under her chin. He sat back, glanced at his wristwatch. Any minute now, Lamont London would arrive, no doubt carrying a full head of steam—and finding Reid Alexander in his daughter's room would do nothing to improve his mood. And Cammi sure didn't need to witness the angry scene, especially not in her condition.

Besides, Reid had promised to drive Billy and Martina to Fort Worth later. He'd called several times to report on Cammi's condition, and they'd rescheduled Billy's appointment for that evening. "I'll check on you soon," he promised, pressing a soft kiss to her temple.

He couldn't help but wonder about the affectionate little gestures he'd been doling out to Cammi, almost from the moment they'd met. He had never been physically demonstrative, not even with people he knew well and loved with all his heart.

In the doorway, he stopped for one last glance. She looked like a vision, thick black lashes dusting her lightly freckled cheeks, satiny hair spilling across her pillow like a mahogany halo. He could think of only one word to describe her: *Beautiful*…inside and out. She was everything he'd ever wanted in a woman. On the rare occasions when he allowed himself to dream of a wife and a houseful of kids, it was a woman like Cammi he pictured at his side, sharing life's ups and downs.

He wished he could be here, holding her hand, when the doc came back to deliver the sorry news about the baby. But Reid had a far bigger regret than that.

Soon she'd put two and two together, and when she realized *he'd* been the other driver in the accident that killed her mother, he'd be lucky if she didn't hate him.

"Sweet dreams, pretty lady," he whispered sadly. "God knows you deserve them."

One thing was certain…*his* dreams tonight sure wouldn't be sweet.

Cammi didn't know how much time had passed since Reid brought her to the hospital. She only knew it felt as if she'd gone thirteen rounds in a boxing match. Blindfolded. With her hands tied behind her back.

Everything ached, from the soles of her feet to her scalp. Squinting, she rested a palm on her stomach. *Father,* she quietly prayed with a lump in her throat,

watch over us and protect us. Despite her fervent
prayer, deep down she feared her baby was already
lost to her.

Reid had watched over them, Cammi admitted.
She'd always taken pride at not being the clingy,
needy type, but she didn't remember needing anyone
more than she'd needed Reid today. If she hadn't
been so exhausted, she could thank him now for all
he'd done. But she'd gone and fallen asleep, and
while she was off in dreamland, he'd taken her at her
word, and left.

She'd roused enough, there at the end of his visit,
to remember the way he'd said goodbye. His tone had
confused her, because he'd sounded as if he'd never
see her again. Not that she could blame him, all things
considered. *Big handsome guy like that,* Cammi
thought, *deserves better than the likes of me.*

Even the simple act of running a hand through her
hair reminded her of him, of how he'd gently tucked
a curl behind her ears, brushed the bangs from her
eyes. She stared at her left hand, thinking of the way
he'd kissed each knuckle…all but her ring finger, that
is. And was it any wonder? What man in his right
mind would deliberately saddle himself with a woman
who carried such heavy burdens.

Dr. Lucas walked into the room just then, white lab
coat flapping behind him, stethoscope clacking
against the pen in his lapel pocket. "Mrs. Carlisle,"
he said, kindly extending his hand. "Remember
me?"

She'd been pretty out of it when he introduced himself before surgery, but yes, she had a vague recol-
lection. Cammi nodded and shook his hand. "Thanks

for stopping by, Doctor. I was just wondering about…things.''

He dragged the chair beside her bed closer, spun it around and sat, forearms resting on its back. ''How much do you recall of what I told you outside the operating room?'' he asked, laying her chart on the night table.

''Not much, I'm afraid.''

Lucas nodded. ''Well, let me go over it again. For starters, everything looks fine. Your D-and-C went very well and—''

''D-and-C?'' Cammi's heartbeat quickened. She grabbed the bed controls, pushed the raise backrest button. ''So, it's true, then?'' Tears stung her eyes. ''I lost the baby?''

Nodding gravely, Lucas said, ''I'm afraid so.'' He leaned forward. ''But there wasn't a thing you could have done to prevent it. Most people have no idea how common miscarriages are. It's no consolation, I know, but it might help some to know that ten percent of all pregnancies end sometime between the seventh and twelfth week.''

He'd been right. The information did absolutely nothing to console her. ''But I fell this morning, and last night I was involved in a minor traffic accident.…''

''Fact is, by the time a miscarriage begins, the baby has already been lost for quite some time.'' Shaking his head, Lucas added, ''Neither your fall nor your accident is responsible for this. One of the hardest things about miscarriage is that most of the time, there's no clue as to the cause.''

He grabbed her file, flipped to the second page.

"We ran the whole battery of tests on you, starting with a transvaginal ultrasound and HCG to confirm you were, indeed, pregnant, CBC to determine the amount of blood loss, WBC to rule out potential infections. The D-and-C was mostly precautionary, because remaining tissue can cause infection."

Lucas turned to another page, then met her eyes. "Everything looks completely normal, so I can assure you there's no reason you can't have another child…when you're ready, of course." He tapped a fingertip on the clipboard. "And let me stress that there is *no* reason to expect anything like this might happen again."

Another baby? Cammi hadn't even come to grips yet with losing this one. At the moment, she wanted nothing more than to be alone, to think and pray about…about *every*thing.

"Mind if I ask you a personal question?"

Unable to trust her voice, Cammi shook her head.

"That guy who brought you in—is he your husband?"

Another head shake. "Friend," she said. "He's just…a friend."

"Has anyone notified your husband?"

She took a deep breath, released it slowly. "My husband died in a car accident four months ago. In California."

Lucas's eyes widened. "I'm so sorry, very sorry." Standing, he put the chair back where he'd found it, tucked her file under his arm. "Is there anyone I can call for you? Anything I can do?"

"Nothing, thanks. My father is on his way." He should be here by now. He must be stuck in traffic.

He dug around the oversize pocket on his lab coat, withdrew a business card. "If there's anything, anything at all I can do to help…"

Cammi accepted the card, knowing even before he released it that she wouldn't call. "Thanks," she said again.

"Have they brought you anything to eat?"

She answered with a question of her own. "Will you be signing release forms now?"

"In the morning. I want to keep you overnight for observation."

"Whatever you say, Doctor."

He made a note on her file and recapped his pen. "You're to take it real easy for a week or so. I mean it. Nothing strenuous. That means no laundry, no vacuuming, no lifting anything heavier than a five-pound bag of sugar." Lucas started for the door. "And have someone go to the pharmacy," he said over his shoulder, "to pick you up some iron tablets. You lost a lot of blood and need to build yourself up again."

"Okay."

"And no stairs. At least for the first few days."

"But my room is—"

His wagging forefinger reminded Cammi of a metronome. "Uh-uh-uh. 'No stairs' means *no stairs.* Camp out on the couch until Wednesday or Thursday."

Then she remembered the school, and Principal Gardner. "I'm supposed to start a new job on Monday!"

"Out of the question. Do that, and you'll be right back in here by lunchtime, needing a transfusion…or worse."

Feelings of helpless frustration overcame her.

"I'll want to see you in two weeks," Lucas said, half in, half out of the room. "I'll have my nurse give you a call to schedule an appointment."

What else could go wrong? she wondered as the doctor disappeared around the corner.

He hadn't been gone a full minute when her father clomped into the room on well-worn cowboy boots. "What in tarnation is going on around here?" he said, tossing his dusty Stetson onto the foot of her bed.

Careful what you ask for, Cammi thought wryly, *'cause you might just get it.*

Halfway into the seven-hour trip to Fort Worth, Billy yawned and stretched. Digging in the sack of treats Reid had brought, he pulled out a candy bar and clucked his tongue. "You drive like an old man, you know that, son?"

Reid glanced at the dashboard, noted he'd been traveling at exactly the posted limit. *Should've seen me a couple of hours ago,* Reid thought, remembering his trip to the hospital, when he discovered the pickup could actually go the hundred twenty miles per hour promised by the speedometer. "If obeying the law makes me an old man, I've been old since I was fourteen."

"Hmm," Billy teased around a mouthful of chocolate. "That reminds me—the west fields need some fertilizer...." He laughed, then added, "You can't kid a kidder, kid. I remember the way you used to drive that ancient green tractor of mine. Why, even the chickens knew to head for the henhouse when you climbed onto the seat of that monster!"

"True enough," Reid said, chuckling, "but that was different. I never drove the tractor on the highway."

"Speaking of highways, how far is it to Fort Worth, anyway?"

"Three hundred fifty miles, give or take." He glanced at the dashboard clock. "I reckon we'll roll into town just in the nick of time for your appointment."

Billy blew a stream of air through his teeth. "Seven and a half hours on the road, and for what?" he grumbled.

"God willing," Martina said from the back seat, "for a new medication or treatment that will save your life. Or, as you're so fond of saying, 'to save your ornery hide.'"

Turning to face her, he winked. "Guess I could at least *act* a mite grateful, eh?"

In the rearview mirror, Reid saw her blow Billy a kiss, saw the love beaming from her eyes. The sight made him smile, despite the traumatic morning, despite the long trip ahead…and the reason for this outing, because this couple was proof positive that happy marriages did exist. "I'd like to see a reporter from one of those women's magazines interview you guys," he said offhandedly.

"Interview us?" Billy faced front, eyes widened in disbelief. "What in thunderation for?"

Martina clucked her tongue. "William, please watch your language," she said, gently tapping his shoulder with the blunt end of a knitting needle. To Reid, she said, "It's a good question, though—why would a reporter want to interview *us?*"

Reid shrugged. "You've been married—what, a hundred fifty years, yet you're still billing and cooing like young lovebirds."

"Thirty-five years," Martina corrected.

"Only *seems* like a hundred fifty," Billy put in.

She gave him another light rap on the shoulder.

"Jiminy Cricket," he said, laughing. "You didn't let me finish. I was about to add, 'living with me.'"

She giggled quietly. "Lies paint a dark spot on our souls, you know."

"Oh, I don't mind," Billy said. "The Good Lord already knows I'm a tad 'dotty.'"

Reid frowned. "Is that in the Bible?"

Martina lifted her chin. "No, it isn't. But since my beloved granny said it, and my wonderful mama repeated it, there must be some truth to it." She paused, then changed the subject. "Hard to believe we've been together that long, and most of them happy years, at that."

"Most?" Billy put in, heaving a huge fake sigh.

She leaned forward to muss his hair. "Yes, 'most.' Because *mostly,* you're willing to compromise, to talk things out, to negotiate. That's why marriage to you has been easy. Mostly."

"No, it's been easy because you're wonderful."

She giggled again. "No, because *you're* wonderful."

Reid had heard it all before, enough times to know that once they got the old "who's best" ball rolling, it could go on and on. "This meeting of the Mutual Admiration Society has concluded," he droned. He didn't put any stock in Martina's notions about lies darkening the soul, but he sure did hope there was truth to the reasons she'd listed for their successful marriage. He'd always considered himself fair-minded and reasonable, so if he ever found the right girl…

If he found the right girl? Reid believed he *had* found her. Didn't make sense, being so sure about something that important in such a short time. But it would take a miracle to get "the right girl" to forgive him for her mother's death.

What would Cammi be doing right now? he wondered. Sleeping peacefully, he hoped. If she were his wife, she wouldn't need for anything, ever. He'd take two jobs, three if he had to, to provide anything her heart desired. He had a feeling it wouldn't be hard…meeting her heart's desires. She had an easy way about her that told him she'd be happy and satisfied with only the barest of necessities, provided her loved ones' needs were being met. She didn't seem the type to be impressed by mansions, imported furniture or fancy sports cars.

Imagine how good it would feel, he thought, being greeted by the likes of that smile after a long, hard day. He pictured Cammi, taking his arm, leading him to his favorite easy chair, where she'd snuggle into his lap to hear about his day. He could tell by the way she'd leaned into the conversation at Georgia's the night of the accident for her, listening was a fine-honed skill.

Frowning, Reid pursed his lips. He'd never gone boots-over-Stetson for a woman before, not even the most gorgeous and willing of them—and there had been plenty, like Amanda, who'd dogged his heels around the rodeo circuit. So why did he feel this way about Cammi, a woman he'd only just met?

No similarity between her and his own mother, whose loud, boisterous behavior so often shamed and humiliated him. In many ways she seemed more like Martina.

You're an idiot, Alexander, he chided himself. Her husband had only been gone a few months, and—

Husband. It surprised him, the way his fingers tightened on the steering wheel and his jaw clenched at the very thought of her sharing any portion of her life with another man. He tried to shake off the unthinkable thought. *Mind on the road,* he told himself. *Mind on the road…*

"What's going through that handsome head of yours?" Martina asked.

He met her eyes in the rearview mirror and forced a grin. "Just concentrating on the drive, is all."

"Nonsense," she countered. "A man doesn't grind down his molars and grimace because he's reading road signs and avoiding potholes."

Billy chuckled. "Well, I'll give you my two cents' worth. He's buildin' castles in the air about that li'l gal he crashed into."

Reid feigned a look of exasperation. "Two cents is about all that theory is worth. Here's an idea—go on back to sleep and save talk like that for—"

Billy laughed. "What's that old saying? 'Methinketh the cowboy protesteth too mucheth.'"

"Good thing there isn't a law against butchering Shakespeare," Reid pointed out, "'cause you just massacred that line."

Martina leaned forward, excited about some wildflower or other growing alongside the road. Thankfully, Billy seemed interested in the scenery, too, pointing out tree species and shrubbery the state had planted in the last "Beautify Texas" campaign.

Reid had managed to sidetrack them—this time— but he knew he'd better be more careful about where he did his daydreaming from now on, especially when it involved Cammi Carlisle.

Which might be tricky, considering how often and how deeply she filled his thoughts.

Reid would have given anything to hear the same silly banter going home as he'd endured on the drive to Fort Worth, even if it meant putting up with talk of his having a "thing" for Cammi Carlisle. But the specialist who'd examined Billy last night agreed with all the others:

Billy had Amyotrophic Lateral Sclerosis.

ALS.

And there was no known cure.

When the doctor in Amarillo first diagnosed the illness, Reid wanted to learn about the disease that might kill his best friend, his father figure, his mentor. Trips to the library and hours searching Internet Web sites made him yearn for those days when his only knowledge of ALS was that it had taken the life of baseball great Lou Gehrig.

In a horribly predictable fashion, the slight muscle weakness that sent Billy to the doctor in the first place quickly progressed, stealing finger dexterity and making it impossible for him to continue stringing the colorful, long-plumed fishing lures he'd been creating for years at the request of friends and neighbors.

Thanks to ALS, there'd be no more going off at dawn, fishing all by himself; twitching limbs and muscle spasms could cause him to lose his balance and topple out of his one-man johnboat.

Things would worsen gradually over these next few months, sapping Billy's strength and dignity until, one by one, every major organ stopped doing its job.

Now, as Billy leaned against the passenger window pretending to be asleep, as Martina's knitting needles click-clacked fast enough to create sparks, Reid wished he could reach out to them, wished there was something he could do or say to bring them comfort. But since the one thing they needed to hear— "cure"—was an impossibility, he held his silence.

For a reason he couldn't explain, he wanted Cammi near. It made no sense, and he felt selfish for so much as thinking that she could comfort *him,* especially after all she'd been through. Still, something told him if she knew the details about Billy's illness, if she knew how much the man meant to Reid, she'd shelve her own troubles to help him bear up under his.

On the other hand, being a devout Christian, Cammi would likely ply him with a list of Bible verses and prayers. He didn't cotton to getting into a verbal sparring match with a good, churchgoing gal about the existence of God *or* His presence in their day-to-day lives.

It would be hours yet, before he delivered Billy and Martina back to the Rockin' C Ranch, and since dawn had just broken it was too early to call Cammi. He'd barely slept a wink, lying on that too-soft hotel mattress, wondering how she was doing, wondering if her doctor had released her from the hospital and how she'd taken the news of the miscarriage. He could only hope that whatever was wrong between her and Lamont could be set aside until Cammi was her strong, healthy self again.

He wanted to hear her voice. No, *needed* to hear it, if for no other reason than to prove she'd made it through the night all right. As soon as he got the hands started on their next chore, he'd take five minutes and give her a call. He'd start out by apologizing for not being there when she woke up, for not being there to hold her hand when the doctor came in.

Reasonable or not, for the first time in his life, he intended to do what felt *right,* rather than what made sense. That meant 'fessing up, admitting he'd been the one driving the pickup that awful night. If she didn't slap him silly, maybe there was hope for them.

Maybe.

He knew this: He had to *try.*

Chapter Five

"I promise to tell you everything," Cammi said, "the minute we get home."

By the time Lamont had arrived at the hospital the day before, she'd been sleeping comfortably, thanks to the mild sedative the nurse had given her. She'd given the hospital staff strict instructions not to reveal anything to her father about her condition so Lamont had no choice but to go home and wait till this morning to find out why she'd been hospitalized.

Lamont's brow furrowed, a sure sign his patience was wearing thin. "You think I can't handle some ugly news?" He tossed the plastic bag he'd been carrying onto her tray table.

"It's not about what you can handle, Dad, it's—"

He took his hat from the foot of her bed and, holding it by the brim, spun it round and round like a disconnected steering wheel. "It's no secret that hospitals give me the heebie-jeebies."

True enough. He'd gone through a mighty rough spell after Rose's death. While he holed up in his den with a bottle of whiskey, Cammi took charge. She started by gathering the ranch hands to explain that they hadn't been paid because her dad was "under the weather." Handing the foreman the ranch checkbook, she instructed him to do what her father would...until Lamont was ready to do it himself.

She'd helped her mother enough to know how everything else should be done. And so she did it, from packing lunches and readying her sisters to catch the school bus, to monitoring their homework. It had been her fault, after all, that Rose had been out that night in the first place; if Cammi hadn't needed a new dress to wear for her solo in the Harvest Days show at her school, Rose would have been home, safe and sound, that terrible, rainy night.

So Cammi didn't complain when her friends went to the mall or to the movies on weekends while she cleaned, did laundry, cooked suppers that could be frozen and heated in the oven on weeknights. Nothing pleased her more than when she was able to coax her bleary-eyed father to eat a few bites of something healthy every evening. Because if it hadn't been for her silly girlish vanity, if she'd been satisfied wearing one of the dozens of dresses already in her closet, he'd still have had his beloved Rose.

When the food supply ran low, Cammi scoured the house for loose change and dollar bills and, stash in hand, phoned Rose's best friend. Nadine did more than deliver staples that day; she sat Lamont down and reminded him what Rose would have expected of him. From that day forward, he'd done his duty—and then some. But his aversion to hospitals hadn't changed one whit. Cammi could use a bit of Nadine's commonsense wisdom right about now.

"If something is wrong with you, I want to hear about it," Lamont said, sliding a forefinger round and round under his suede hatband.

"There's nothing wrong with me...." She hoped and prayed that was true, because someday, she wanted a houseful of children.

"Person doesn't wind up in a place like this if nothing's wrong."

"I know, I know. And I promise to tell you everything once we're home. For now, let's just say it's nothing serious. Okay?"

Lamont sat the hat on the foot of her bed again. "Let's have a look at you...." He lifted her chin on a bent forefinger. Grinning, he said, "Good golly, Miss Molly. You look like something the dog drug in."

"Then, it's a good thing I'm not thinking of entering the Miss Texas pageant, eh?"

"Hogwash. You'd win, hands down, even after..." He paused. "...after whatever put you in this rotten place."

He handed her the plastic bag. "Thought you might need a change of clothes. Hope I did okay, putting an outfit together."

Cammi peeked inside, where a neatly folded sweatsuit lay nestled on her underthings. She had a hard time blinking back tears of gratitude. "It's perfect," she told him, climbing out of bed.

Lamont nodded. "I'll just wait in the hall while

you get out of that foul thing they call a hospital gown."

"So you can be closer to the main entrance?"

He grinned slightly. "Main *exit* is more like it."

Despite every effort to stay awake during the half-hour drive back to River Valley, Cammi dozed off half a dozen times. Finally, though, the magnificent ranch house appeared on the horizon.

"Home never looked better," she said, mostly to herself.

He parked the truck out front, and asked as he unlocked the front door, "So what'll you have, coffee or tea?"

One of the nurses had said dehydration went hand in hand with hemorrhaging. "Nice tall glass of water would be great. The air is so dry in that place."

Closing the door behind them, Lamont threw his keys into the burled wooden bowl on the foyer table. Hands on her shoulders, he inspected her face. "You're lookin' mighty pale. Head on into the den and put your feet up. I'll be in soon as I fetch our drinks." He turned her around, gave her a gentle shove toward the doorway.

Cammi started forward, then changed her mind. What she was about to tell him would break his heart, would become one more item on his long "Ways Cammi Has Disappointed Me" list. She might not get a chance to tell him, once the truth was out, how dear he was to her, how very hard she'd been trying these past few months to live in a way that would make him proud, to make up for being the reason Rose was out that night.

She spun on her heels and threw her arms around him. "I love you, Dad. So much that sometimes—"

He kissed the top of her head. "And I love you, too, sweetie, more than words could ever say." Tilting his head back, he gave her another once-over. "Now get on in there," he said, tousling her hair, "and sit down before you fall down."

Nodding, Cammi did as she was told, choosing the end of the deep blue leather couch nearest his favorite chair. Feet resting on the glass-topped coffee table, and huddled under a fringed afghan, she closed her eyes. She didn't know how much time had passed before Lamont walked into the room, carrying a steaming mug of coffee for himself and a glass of ice water for her.

He put the mug on his end table, handed her the tumbler. "You sure you're up to this?" he asked. The black leather of his recliner squeaked in protest as he settled his bulk onto its ample seat. "We can put off…whatever…until later."

Nodding, she sipped the water. The old mantel clock above the fireplace ticked off the seconds as Lamont rested a booted ankle on his knee. Fingers drumming on the chair's worn armrest, he heaved a sigh.

Cammi sat up straighter, put the glass on a soapstone coaster beside the sofa. "There's really no way to ease into this."

Fingers steepled under his chin, Lamont nodded. "Just start at the beginning, sweetie."

She could see by the tired expression on his face that he'd prepared himself for the worst. True to form, she wouldn't disappoint him. And wasn't *that* a bitter irony, she thought; in every way imaginable, she'd let him down, time and time again, but this time...

Clearing her throat, she did as he suggested and started at the beginning, explaining how she'd met Rusty on a movie set. "I'd been hired to play an extra," she said, "and he was a stuntman." She told Lamont how it had been love at first sight—or so she'd thought; how much they seemed to have in common; how much fun they'd had together. "He wasn't a Christian," she continued, "and I knew you wouldn't like that. So I decided to work hard, to pray hard, and when he accepted Jesus as his Lord and Savior, *then* I'd tell you about him and...everything."

Cammi slid past the buying of the marriage license, the ceremony, the honeymoon. It wasn't like Lamont to sit there so quietly. Since Cammi didn't know what to make of it, she plunged on.

"Didn't take long to figure out he'd hardened his heart to the Word." She began fiddling with the afghan's fringe, nervously wrapping it first around one finger, then another. "Then, there were rumors...." She had to stop for a moment, because remembering how humiliating, it had been to hear about Rusty's secret life threatened her precarious hold on self-control. "Turned out they weren't rumors, after all."

She took another sip of water, hoping Lamont wouldn't recognize it as a stall tactic, nothing more. "He'd been gone four straight nights when...when a policeman woke me at three in the morning. He drove me to the morgue, where they showed me..."

Cammi ran both hands through her hair. "He'd crashed his convertible into a tree, impaling himself on the steering column...and injuring his...date."

Lamont's eyebrows lifted as his hands gripped the chair's armrest. "His *date?*"

Cammi nodded. "Weird, huh? Some people think it's perfectly acceptable to have a wife *and* a girl-friend."

Lamont sat on the edge of his chair, elbows resting on his knees. He clasped his hands together and said, "Something tells me there's more...."

"Yes," she whispered, "there's more." *Just say it,* she thought. "Later that same day, my doctor called to say—" Cammi met her father's eyes "—to say I was pregnant."

He hung his head. "I sorta thought that's what you'd say."

He stared at the floor and didn't speak for what seemed to Cammi like an hour. Then he got to his feet and sat beside her on the couch.

"C'mere," Lamont said, drawing her into a hug.

The floodgates opened, releasing all the misery and sadness, all the regret and recrimination she'd been bottling up since that horrible day. It surprised her, when she'd cried it all out, to see tears in her father's eyes, too.

"I'm so sorry, Dad. I hate being such a disappoint-ment to—"

He laid a finger over her lips to silence her. "Shh," he said. "Don't talk that way. You've never been anything but a joy." Holding her at arm's length, he gave her a gentle shake. "You're the spittin' image of your mama, and I'd love you for that alone. God forgive me for saying it, but you're twice the woman she was, twice as smart, twice as thoughtful."

Using the pads of his thumbs, he dried her tears.

"Do you know what she was doing the night she died?"

Cammi nodded. "Shopping for a new dress for me."

"She forgot your dress, darlin'. That was her excuse when she left here that night, but it wasn't in the car after—" He took a deep breath. "I told her not to go out in that weather, but would she listen? *No-o-o.* 'There's a sale at Gizmo's,' she said. 'If I wait till tomorrow, I'll miss all the latest styles!' she said."

He sat back, pulled Cammi with him. "The cops gave me everything they found in her car—cassette tapes, keys, her purse...and four dress boxes from Gizmo's." He held her at arm's length to add, "Did Gizmo's ever sell girls' clothes?"

Cammi shook her head.

"I've been telling you for years the accident wasn't your fault. If I'd known *why* you blamed yourself..." Lamont ran a hand through his hair. "Maybe if I'd been a better father, I would have asked."

"Dad, you—"

"You didn't hold it against me, did you?"

"Hold what against you? You've been the best father a girl could ask for!"

"Y'know," he said, kissing her temple, "I believe you mean that. Which is just one of a thousand reasons I love you like I do. You never gave it a thought, did you, that if I hadn't been so wrapped up in my own self-pity, I might have asked—"

"Dad, really. Stop saying things like—"

"And look at you now, not an hour out of the hospital and trying to excuse my bad behavior. You're something else, you know that? You'd never put your life at risk for something so trivial as a sale on dresses, and the proof is the way you handled things after your mama's funeral.''

She remembered only too well that at first, he'd held it together. It was later, after the friends stopped dropping by and the in-laws stopped calling, when the casserole dishes had been reclaimed and the flowers had all dried up, that he'd let grief and despair claim him….

''If she'd died for any other reason, I could have handled it. It would've hurt like mad, but…*dresses?* Pretty clothes were more important to her than staying safe for her family?'' He gave Cammi another gentle shake. ''Don't you see, sweetie? I'll love her till the day I die, but I can't forgive her for making you girls motherless, for making me a widower. I've never been disappointed in you—it's *her* I'm disappointed in!'' One last shake before he let her go. ''And let's not forget that if you hadn't stepped in, run things while I was havin' myself a pity party, we might've lost everything. You saved our bacon, Camelia.''

Cammi tried to take it all in.

''Well,'' Lamont said on a heavy sigh, ''at least it's all out in the open now.''

''No, not all of it, Dad. There's one more thing….''

''I know. You lost the baby.''

His voice was flat, unemotional, when he said it, as if he couldn't bear to say it any other way.

She felt the tears begin to well up again. Unable to trust herself to speak, Cammi nodded. When she found her voice, she said, ''I didn't love Rusty, not the way a wife should love her husband, but I wanted this baby. Wanted it very much.'' The reasons poured out even faster than her tears—how the child had turned her from a dreamy-eyed girl to a feet-on-the-ground woman, how she'd made solid, rational decisions for the first time in her life for no reason other than that she *had* to behave responsibly from now on, for the baby's sake.

She didn't tell her father about the handsome cowboy she'd met, who'd been her hero in every sense of the word, who'd somehow managed to steal her heart in just a few days. Admitting she was falling in love with him, already, was the same as admitting every other good thing she'd done lately had been a mistake. Besides, there didn't seem to be much point in telling him about Reid, because what chance did she have for a future with the man who she suspected had been driving the other car that night!

"You've been making responsible decisions since you were twelve, sweetie. And you'll go right on making them. God has blessed you with—"

Cammi didn't hear anything after *God*. Anger deafened her, rage blinded her. She was suddenly keenly aware that God had let her down, big time. She'd done it all by the book, right down to keeping her promise to remain a virgin until her wedding night…and in a city like Hollywood, no less! She'd started every day with a devotional, ended each by reading His Word. It hadn't been easy, what with her wacky waitress schedule, but she'd found a church and hadn't missed a single Sunday service. Despite the ugly rumors that surfaced after Rusty's death, she hadn't given in to the temptation to hate him. Rather, she'd decided early on to tell the baby nothing but good things about its daddy. She'd never asked the Almighty for anything but the strength to do His Will, and yet He'd taken the baby. He'd—

"Sweetie," Lamont was saying, "what's wrong? You're white as a bedsheet."

"I'm fine. Just a little tired, maybe."

"Why not go up to bed and take a nap, then, while I rustle us up something to eat."

"Can't. Doc says I'm not to use the stairs for a few days," she muttered. "Need some iron tablets, too, and I can't start my new job for at least a week."

"New job?"

With everything that had happened, Cammi hadn't found time to tell him about her new teaching position. "Puttman Elementary. Fourth grade," she said dully. "I was supposed to start on Monday."

"Well, I'm sure the principal will understand."

No doubt he would. Mr. Garner had seemed like a nice enough fellow. Which wasn't the point at all. Having something to do would help put the miscarriage to the back of her mind, would keep her occupied.

"I'll scrounge up some bed linens," Lamont said, standing. "You'll sleep right here till your doctor gives you the green light."

Cammi nodded.

"Mind telling me who it was that called me from the hospital?"

"As it turns out, he's the guy I crashed into last night. I ran into him again in town, after my meeting with the Puttman principal, when…" She remembered Amanda, remembered losing her footing on the corner, tumbling into the street, Reid's big strong arms steadying her. "He was there when…"

"Good, you have his name and address, then. I need to thank him for getting you to the hospital safely, for staying with you till he knew I was on my way."

Cammi knew a gift wouldn't be necessary or expected, not with a man like Reid, and said so.

"Reid?"

"Reid Alexander. He used to be an award-winning rodeo cowboy, and now he works as the Rockin' C foreman."

Lamont put his back to her. "I know perfectly well who he is." The hard edge to his voice told her Reid was indeed the boy who'd been driving that night.

As if he'd read her mind, Lamont said, "Besides, he's a cowboy, and cowboys are trouble. I oughta know." He looked over his shoulder. "When this accident mess is cleaned up, I want you to keep your distance from him."

Hearing those words hurt.

"Trust me," Lamont added. "I know what I'm talking about. Stay away from the likes of him."

For a moment after he left the room, she asked herself what had happened to give him such a negative mind-set toward all cowboys. He had a few kinks in his armor, but self-righteousness and judgmentalism weren't among them. Especially considering he himself had been a cowboy all his life!

Maybe Lily knew the answer to that question. And maybe Cammi's little sister would gather up some old movies—comedies, preferably, and novels, too… books with plots that had nothing whatsoever to do with love and marriage and babies. Because if she didn't find something to occupy her mind while she recuperated, she'd end up feeling sorry for herself. And that was the last thing she wanted, or could afford, to do.

Weird the way the mind works, Cammi thought, because the mere mention of love and marriage and babies made her think of Reid. *Again.* He'd said he had to drive his boss to see a specialist about controlling Billy's ALS. He'd probably be halfway home by now, hopefully with good news. Maybe after her nap, she'd give Reid a call, see how things turned out.

And maybe you won't, she thought.

Lily sat on the arm of the sofa and held out the phone. "Some guy wants to talk to you."

"Mechanic, probably," Cammi said, putting the receiver to her ear. She felt much better after her long nap. "Hello?"

"Cammi, hi. It's Reid. Just thought I'd call to see how you were doing."

She felt herself blush and tried to turn away so Lily wouldn't see it. "I'm...I'm fine. And your boss? How's he?"

There was a considerable pause before he said, "Not so hot."

Another pause, then, "How 'bout I buy you a cup of coffee in town?"

"Sorry, I'm confined to quarters for the better part of a week. I'd invite you to come here, but..."

Before she had a chance to make up an excuse,

Reid interrupted with "Maybe some other time, then."

"Maybe."

"So, what did your doctor say?"

Cammi filled him in, spelling out the doctor's orders while being careful not to mention the miscarriage; she hadn't had a chance to fill Lily in yet.

"Wish I'd been there when Dr. Lucas told you about…you know, the uh…"

It touched her that he was having a hard time saying "miscarriage." "I wish you'd been there, too." He had no idea how much she'd wished it! But it was probably for the best that he'd left before the doctor showed up. Reid already had more than enough reason to avoid her without witnessing the blue funk she'd slipped into after hearing the news.

"Well, guess I'll let you go. You need your rest."

"Right." A couple of days ago, she'd have said "I'll pray for your boss." Well, a lot of things were different now. "Good luck to your boss."

"He's been more like a father to me than a boss," Reid said, "but I appreciate the sentiment, anyway." And then he chuckled.

"What."

"You surprised me, that's all."

"How?"

"I thought for sure you'd say something like 'I'll keep him in my prayers.'"

Cammi harrumphed. "Why would I do a silly thing like that? It isn't like He hears anything I say, anyway."

Silence. Then Reid said, "'Course He hears you, Cammi. Why would you say such a thing?"

"Because it's true, that's why." She didn't like the turn of the conversation. Didn't like the angry feelings swirling in her gut…where her baby used to be. "Well, I appreciate your call," she said, hoping he'd take the hint and hang up.

"No problem. Mind if I check in on you again soon?"

"It's a free country." *Get a grip, Cammi,* she told herself. It's *God* you're mad at, so why take it out on Reid?

"Get some rest," he said again. "Talk to you later."

She had barely hung up when Lily said, "Who was *that?*"

Cammi pretended to be engrossed in adjusting the hem of her pajama top. "The guy from the other night."

Lily grinned. "Car Crash Cowboy, y'mean?"

"None other."

"Care to explain why I didn't hear any talk about insurance companies or mechanics or body shops?"

She was wiggling her eyebrows when Cammi looked up. Might as well get it over with, she thought. "Have a seat, kiddo," she said, patting the cushion beside her. "I have a story to tell you."

"Is this the one about the husband named Rusty who died in a convertible with his girlfriend?"

Cammi couldn't believe her ears.

"Close your mouth, big sister. We don't need a flycatcher."

She snapped her teeth together. "There are no flies in Texas this time of year, anyway." She slapped the couch again. "Now, have a seat and tell me how you know so much."

"Oh, let's just say a little bird told me."

Lamont wasn't the type who would have told her, so—

"Stop trying so hard to figure it out." Lily giggled. "I can almost see the smoke comin' out of your ears!"

Cammi gasped, feigned shock. "You were *eavesdropping!* Shame on you, Lily!"

Her cheeks flushed. "No, I wasn't," she said. "At least, not at first. I was diddy-boppin' down the hall when I heard voices. By the time I figured out who was talking…and about what…it was too late to backtrack. Sounded so serious, so important that I didn't want to interrupt."

Cammi sighed. "Well, it's actually a relief. I didn't relish having to repeat it all, anyway."

Lily scooted closer, slung an arm over Cammi's shoulder. "Sorry you had to go through that, sis. Honest. That Rusty was a bum. A no-good, low-down—"

"Wasn't all his fault. I had a part in that mess, too, you know."

"You didn't cheat on your spouse. Worst thing you did was take the word of that stinking—"

"Lily, really…"

"Well," she said, giving Cammi a sideways hug, "I can't help it. For the past few hours I've been stewing over what that jerk did to you." She balled up a fist and shook it in the air. "If he wasn't already dead, I'd hunt him down and kill him myself!"

Cammi turned to face her. "Whoa. Are you sure

you're my baby sister? The one who mothers orphaned calves and rescues critters that would otherwise become roadkill? The same sweet girl who nursed a hawk until it was well enough to fly away home? The gentle soul who cringes when Dad mashes a spider?''

''This is different,'' she huffed. ''We're talkin' *family* here.'' She jabbed a thumb into her chest. ''Anybody messes with my kin whilst I'm around,'' she said in her thickest Texas drawl, ''has got Lily London to answer to!''

Cammi hugged her. ''I love you, too, kiddo.''

''So what's all this anti-God stuff? Never thought I'd see the day when Camelia London would blaspheme the Lord.''

''Wasn't blasphemy,'' Cammi defended. ''I only said… I'm just sick to death of looking to heaven for help and getting nothing but dust in my eye.''

Lily blinked, swallowed and licked her lips. ''Good grief, Cammi, what would Dad say if he heard you talking this way!''

''I have too much respect for him to talk this way in his presence.''

''Well, don't you worry…I'm sure not gonna tell him. I like all my parts right where God put 'em, thank you!'' She coughed. ''Sorry for the *God* reference, what with you bein' *mad* at Him and all.''

''Yeah, I'm mad. Don't I have a right to be? I wanted that baby, even if it did come by way of a low-down, no-good, stinking, cheating jerk! I prayed myself hoarse, trying to make the right decisions for our future. Why, I'll bet there are calluses on my knees, I spent so much time praying for it to be healthy, and happy, and well loved, and cared for, and everything else a baby deserves to be! And what did God do? Nothing, that's what. So yeah, I'm mad. Good and mad. Because what have I ever done in my life that would make Him—''

"Cammi," Lily said softly, "stop it. You're supposed to be resting. You want the bleeding to start up again?''

She took a deep breath, let it out again. "No, of course not," she said, shaking her head.

"You have to give yourself some time, Cammi. Time to let this all sink in. In a couple of days, you're going to feel completely differently about everything. You'll feel—''

"No, I won't. I'll feel exactly the same in a couple of days, in a couple of months. I'll feel that God let me down, is what I'll feel! I'll feel that way because it's true. I wanted this baby, wanted it so very much. And oh, Lily, it breaks my heart that He took it. I miss it, miss it so...."

Until a tear splashed on the back of her hand, Cammi hadn't realized she'd been crying.

Lily gathered her close, patting her back as she whispered, "Hush, now. It's okay. I understand."

But Cammi knew Lily didn't understand. How could she, when she'd never carried a child inside her, never looked forward to feeding time and nursery rhymes and even diaper changing. She'd never planned a nursery, right down to which Mother Goose character would dominate the decorating theme, never held her breath as she anticipated feeling those first fluttering little kicks.

She hoped Lily would never know the fear that

wraps around a mother's heart when the brutal cramping begins, or the terror that goes with seeing your life's blood—and that of your unborn child—pouring out like water from a tap. Hopefully, Lily would never know the heartache of hearing the word *miscarriage*.

Cammi cried until spent, feeling foolish and childish and weak-willed. Which made things all the worse, because she didn't like behaving this way—especially not in front of her youngest sister. What kind of example was that!

She didn't understand it, because she'd never been one to give in to tears, had always controlled her emotions, not the other way around. All her life, she'd looked down her nose at girls and women who got weepy when things didn't go their way. After her mother's death, when her dad fell apart before her eyes, Cammi vowed to be strong, to be in command of herself at all times. She owed him that much.

Were these tears a wake-up call? A lesson in humility from on high? *What do You hope to teach me, Lord,* she demanded silently, *that the poor choices and stupid decisions I've made all my life have been my own unique brand of boo-hooing?*

Anger, she decided, was even more self-destructive than self-pity. She had to get hold of herself, right now, for her own sake as well as for Lily's, for her father's.

Cammi sat up and grabbed a tissue from the dispenser on the coffee table. Blotting her eyes, she said, "Sorry, Lily. Didn't mean to fall apart like that."

"Hey, everybody needs a good cry now and then. It's human. Why else would God have given us…" Lily bit her lip.

"Don't worry, I don't expect you to share my views on You-Know-Who," she said, aiming a thumb at the ceiling.

Lily got to her feet. "Time to feed Elmer the calf. Anything I can get you before I head out to the barn?"

Cammi shook her head. "Nah. I've got everything I need right here." She smiled. "But thanks, kiddo. I love ya."

Lily's "love you, too" echoed in Cammi's mind long after her sister left the room.

Funny, she thought, how this being angry with God seemed to invigorate her. She needed to think about that, figure out why—

The phone's insistent ring interrupted her reverie. She lifted the receiver. "Hello?"

"Cammi. It's me, Reid."

"Again?" she teased.

"Yeah, I had to ask you…are you really okay? You sounded a little strange when I called before."

"My sister was with me. I didn't want her hearing about the—" She straightened her back and lifted her chin, determined not to wallow in self-pity "—miscarriage secondhand." She laughed, a little too long and a little too hard, but what did she care? Reid had already formed his opinions about her—negative ones, no doubt. "Turns out she'd heard the whole story while standing in the hallway as I spelled it out for my dad."

He didn't say anything right away. When he did speak, Reid's deep voice sounded concerned. "So, you're okay, then?"

Mad as a wet hen, but healthy as a horse, she

thought. Odd, but Dr. Lucas hadn't warned her that thinking in clichés was a result of miscarriage.

There, she'd said it again. And she hadn't fallen apart saying it. Trick is, she realized, not to avoid it, but to say it over and over and over. *Miscarriage, miscarriage, miscarriage…*

Nope. That wasn't going to work. And the proof was the hard knot that had formed in her throat.

"Cammi?"

She took a sip of water. "I'm here."

"I sure would like to see you."

You would? But why?

"Soon as you're up to it, I want to take you to dinner. Someplace nice, where we can talk."

It was too soon after Rusty's demise to think of it as an official date. And her father had flat-out forbidden her to see Reid—romantically, she presumed. But there was no reason under the sun they couldn't be friends, right?

"Tell you what," Reid was saying. "When you're feeling better, give me a call and we'll set it up."

He'd been so easy to lean on yesterday. If only he knew how easy.

"Cammi?"

"Sorry," she said, free hand rubbing her temple. "Sounds like a plan to me." She couldn't imagine calling him to "set things up," but being rude to the guy hardly seemed necessary. Like Lily said, time would pass, and as it did, Reid would forget he'd made the offer.

"Talk to you soon, then?"

"Yeah, soon."

Not, she thought, hanging up. Reid was a great guy.

Too great. In just a few days, he'd succeeded in making her fall for him, like some silly schoolgirl with a crush on her high school's quarterback. Well, she was too old and too wise to go down that road again. If Rusty hadn't taught her anything else, he'd taught her that!

Suddenly, Cammi felt sleepy again. Lying back among the pillows Lamont had brought her, she closed her eyes.

And despite all her tough talk, Reid's handsome face carried her off to dreamland, where they sat side by side on a wide, covered porch, rocking a child in the cradle between them....

That evening Reid lay on his back, fingers linked behind his neck, staring at the shadowy blades of the ceiling fan above his head. Something hadn't set well with him about that phone call to Cammi. He'd come to expect a certain melodious quality to play in her voice. Surely everything that had happened would tone the music down some—but that much?

He'd been tossing and turning for hours now, wondering about it. Had he been wrong about her being spunky and tough? Was she an average woman, after all, with no special ability to roll with the punches, take life on the chin? He didn't think so. He'd met her under nerve-racking circumstances, and if what she'd gone through earlier didn't count as "stressful," Reid didn't know what did.

It was that reference to God, more than anything else, that got him to wondering, because she'd seemed to him a rock-solid believer, a live-life-by-the-Good-Book kind of gal. He felt that way in part because she'd said things like "I'll pray for Billy" and "Pray with me, Reid," and in part because he didn't think a person was born resilient, and Cammi was one of the most iron-willed people he'd ever met. Stuff like that didn't fall out of the sky; it was built into a body by dint of hard work, and prayer, and, yes, faith.

Hearing her talk like that about the Almighty, well, it rattled him. *He* didn't have faith because God had never answered a single prayer he'd prayed. Maybe, like one of the Old Testament verses said, he was paying for the sins of his parents, neither of whom had lived a model Christian life. And maybe, he simply hadn't earned God's attention. Cammi, on the other hand, *had* earned it. Virtue all but glowed in her big brown eyes. He took comfort in the fact that people like Martina and Billy—and Cammi—had developed lasting relationships with the Almighty; it gave him hope that someday, if he kept his nose to the grindstone long enough, even the likes of him could have God's ear!

Besides, Cammi seemed to take such comfort from believing the Lord actually listened to her prayers. That knowledge gave her the confidence to be wide open and accepting, to be fearless. It's what made her happier, more grounded than most, and—

At a horrible thought, Reid sat upright in bed. Now that she'd put his name together with the rodeo, could she have found out what kind of life he'd led on the circuit? Had she seen him for the many-flawed man that he was? Had she judged him too big a sinner to be worthy of her time?

No, Cammi didn't strike him as self-righteous. He'd only known her for a few days, but Reid already felt as if he knew her well. If the eyes are the windows to the soul, he thought, Cammi was good to the bone. And he ought to know; he'd spent hours looking into those chocolate-brown eyes. Even now, the memory of them made his stomach flip.

Something else had to explain her mood....

Then he remembered the despair that drove many a good mare mad. Depression would explain the dullness in her voice, explain her anger at God, too. And who had more reason to slump into a blue mood than Cammi, who'd so recently become a widow, who'd just lost her first child?

On his feet now, Reid began pacing. He kept it up for a minute or two, then stopped midstep. Hadn't she said the doctor ordered a week's worth of R and R? And hadn't she told him "no stairs allowed"?

Reid got dressed in the dark and hurried down the stairs, carrying his boots in one hand, his Stetson in the other. In the kitchen, he dashed off a quick note to let Martina and Billy know where they could find him—and headed for River Valley Ranch.

Chapter Six

Reid pressed his forehead to a pane in the French doors and watched as Cammi put down her magazine and grabbed the remote. She wore a white terry-cloth robe with bright blue butterflies on the pockets, and slippers to match. He smiled, thinking she looked adorable with her thick dark hair gathered up in a swingy ponytail—like a high school girl at a slumber party.

She flicked through the stations twice before settling on a black-and-white movie featuring Humphrey Bogart and Ingrid Bergman. Strange, Reid thought, how he'd seen five minutes of that film here, ten minutes there, without ever watching it from beginning to end. He was wondering if Cammi would settle in to enjoy the whole thing, when she lifted her arms overhead and stretched, reminding him of the cougar he'd seen while traveling with the rodeo, its sleek, well-toned body reaching high on the trunk of a scrub pine to work out the kinks in its back and signal competitors that she was a beast to be reckoned with. It was quite a sight to behold. And *Cammi* was a sight to behold, too.

The day before, they'd shared something few people have, something that forever changed their relationship from whatever it *had been* to… He shrugged. He didn't know how to define what they'd been, what they were now to one another, but he knew this: He wanted her in his life from now on.

Woolgathering like that had been what prompted him to get out of bed, throw on some clothes and head to River Valley Ranch in the middle of the night. During the drive over, he'd argued with himself: Would he be sorry for dropping by unannounced? Or would things turn out as he hoped? Well, he was here now, gawking into her den like a peeping Tom; might as well go for broke, find out once and for all what they meant to each other.

Not wanting to scare her, Reid pecked his fingernails lightly on the glass. Immediately, she hit the remote's mute button and sat up, searching out the source of the sound. After a second or two, she looked over her shoulder and directly at him. Or so it seemed. He shivered involuntarily, though he knew she couldn't possibly see him with the backdrop of night having turned the interior windows into black mirrors.

"You really *are* obnoxious," she said, flinging the door open.

"Sorry," he whispered hoarsely, "didn't mean to wake you."

"I wasn't sleeping." Cammi tightened the belt of her robe, tugged at its wide collar. "I thought you were the dog."

"You wouldn't be the first li'l gal to call me that," he said, grinning.

Apparently, Cammi didn't appreciate his middle-of-the-night attempt at humor. She stared hard at him for a long moment. "How long have you been out there?" she said at last.

"Minute or two, I reckon." He rubbed his hands together. "Mind if I come in, take the chill off?"

She hesitated, then nodded, and Reid stepped inside. It didn't escape his notice that, before closing the door behind him, she checked the mantel clock. He was wondering how long it would be before she mentioned the time as she perched on the sofa arm.

"Whatever were you thinking, coming here at this hour?"

He felt even more ridiculous now than he had standing on the deck, staring through the slats in the window blinds. "I, uh…" Reid held out his hands, palms up. "I needed to see for myself that you were okay." He could have said concern for her had kept Cammi on his mind since he'd left the hospital, but the truth was, she'd dominated his thoughts from the moment she'd plowed into him in front of Georgia's Diner.

"I'm fine." She lifted her chin to add, "Wasn't expecting company at this hour, but…"

Then she pursed her lips, and he read it as a sign she didn't want to talk about the miscarriage. At least, not here and now. Best way he knew to change the subject was with small talk, but he'd never been much good at that. "Nice place," he said, nodding as he glanced around.

He expected her to agree, to point out one of the

den's burled-wood antiques, or the massive stone fire-place that dominated an entire wall. Instead, she stood and said, "I was just about to fix myself a cup of tea."

She hadn't invited him to join her, he noted. Just as well, because her doctor had ordered her some serious R and R. "I thought you were supposed to be taking it easy."

Laughing softly, Cammi gestured for him to follow. "Brewing tea isn't exactly heavy labor," she said, padding down a long hall toward the kitchen. She flipped a switch, flooding the room with a pale yellow light. "Regular or herbal?" she added, firing up the teakettle.

He'd lap water from a mud puddle if it allowed him to spend a few more minutes in her company. "Regular. But only if you let me—"

She shot him a you-must-be-kidding look and grabbed two mugs from an overhead cabinet. "Thanks, but since I know where things are, it makes more sense if I do it myself."

Nodding, Reid sat at the white-tiled table and hung an arm over the back of a ladder-backed chair. "Where's your father?"

"Upstairs, asleep."

He'd decided halfway between the Rockin' C and River Valley that not even the risk of a confrontation with Lamont London could keep him away. Memories of that night in the E.R. still echoed loudly in his head, almost as loudly as they had in his dreams. It was a relief to know he wouldn't have to worry about that tonight. At least, he hoped not. "You're not afraid all this gabbing will wake him?"

She dismissed his concern with a wave of her hand. "You're safe...." Grinning mischievously, Cammi tilted her head. "Unless you do something to make me scream."

He'd cut off his own arm before doing anything that would frighten or hurt her! "Don't worry," he said, laughing. "I might be obnoxious, but I'm not dangerous."

She winced at the reminder she'd called him a dog. "Sorry about that," Cammi said, filling their mugs with steaming water. After dropping tea bags into each, she added, "I honestly thought you were Dad's dog...and he really did name the pup Obnoxious, by the way."

It surprised him to learn that Lamont had a sense of humor.

She handed him a mug and a spoon, then pointed out the sugar bowl, nestled on a lazy Susan amid napkins, salt and pepper shakers, Tabasco and steak sauce. "Milk?"

"Nah. I'm a high-test man, all the way."

"I like my coffee black, but put sugar in my tea." She shrugged. "Don't know why."

"Why do you need a reason?"

She studied his face, and he squirmed a bit under her scrutiny. "Dunno," she said after a bit.

Time to change the subject...again. "So, how're you feeling?"

"Deja vu?"

Her answer didn't make a lick of sense, and he said so.

She said, "You asked me that in the den."

She looked adorable, standing there frowning, arms

crossed over her chest, tiny slippered foot tapping on the shiny linoleum. "Guess I did, at that." He took a gulp of tea and decided not to take her bad-tempered mood personally. She'd been through a lot these past few days…these past few *months*. "No need to apologize for bein' cranky. I understand perfectly what—"

Eyes wide, she gasped. "Cranky?"

If he'd given it a minute's thought, he could've chosen a better word. "Well, not *cranky,* exactly," he began. "Maybe just—"

Clucking her tongue, Cammi rolled her eyes. "Sorry. Didn't realize I sounded so…so…prickly."

"I'm sure if I came callin' at a respectable hour, you'd be your usual good-spirited self."

"So how's your father figure-slash-mentor-slash-boss?"

He had to hand it to her; she'd changed the subject far more smoothly than he had. Pity was, she'd chosen a subject he'd just as soon avoid. It was hard enough knowing Billy wouldn't be with them much longer, without being asked to admit it out loud. "Poorly, to put it mildly."

"Sorry to hear that."

And he knew she meant it because sympathy glowed in her dark eyes, echoed in her voice. Reid could have kissed her for that. *All in good time,* he cautioned.

"At first, the docs thought it would take a couple of years for the ALS to…" He couldn't bring himself to say *kill him*. "Billy's provin' 'em wrong at every turn, 'cause every day, he's twice as bad as the day before."

"Before I left for the rodeo circuit, I used to see him and Martina fairly often at church services and socials. The kids used to call him Gentle Ben, because hard as he tried to act like a tough old bird, he could never quite pull it off. The things he did for the Children's Center are proof he has a heart even bigger than the Rockin' C." Cammi shook her head and sighed. "How's he handling it?"

He remembered how, not so long ago, Billy could heft bales of hay and bags of feed as if they'd been featherlight. And if Reid had trouble watching him struggle with even the simplest tasks like buttoning his shirt and feeding himself, how much harder must it be for the once-proud and self-sufficient Billy?

"He's doing okay, I reckon, all things considered." Reid ran a fingertip around the rim of his mug. "He wouldn't admit it in a million years, but he's scared."

"And who can blame him?"

"Wish there was something I could do to make life more bearable for him, until…" Though he suspected the end wasn't all that far off, Reid couldn't finish the sentence.

Cammi blinked, sandwiching his hand between her own. "You're already doing it, just by being there for him when he needs you."

She withdrew her hand and stirred her tea. "Must be awfully hard on Martina, too. Those two are like newlyweds, even after all these years together."

My, but she had gorgeous eyes, especially when they got all misty that way. "Mind if I ask you a question?"

"Something tells me I couldn't stop you if I tried."

Chuckling, he shook his head. He loved her sense

of humor, her tendency to put aside her own troubles to focus on the needs of others. There she sat, newly widowed and recuperating from a miscarriage, sincerely concerned about Billy and Martina. "You're something else, Cammi Carlisle, you know that?"

She wrapped both hands around her cup. Did she realize that when she looked down that way, her eyelashes hid the entire top half of her cheek? Or that when she bobbed her head in response to a compliment, it only made him want to pay her another?

The truth started spilling out, things he'd been thinking since the moment they'd met. "Seems I've known you my whole life, as if you've been here, right beside me, for decades. Now tell me, does that make a lick of sense?"

'Course it didn't make sense. Nothing did anymore. Take, for example, the way he couldn't seem to keep his big yap shut in her presence.

She grinned, exposing a deep dimple in her right cheek. Funny, why hadn't he noticed it before? He suppressed an urge to touch it.

"You're pretty easy to be around, too," she said.

Not exactly the response he'd hoped for, but it would do...for now. "So, can I ask you a question?"

"I thought you just did."

He mirrored her grin. "All right, so let me ask another one, then."

She tilted her head, waiting.

"Do you miss him much?"

Again with the big blinkin' brown eyes! If she kept that up, he wouldn't have any choice but to go over there, take her in his arms and—

"Who?"

"Your husband."

Frowning now, Cammi stared at the tabletop again. "I'd rather not talk about Rusty."

Rusty. Moronic name for a grown man, Reid thought. But what he said was "Still hurts pretty bad, huh?"

She shrugged one shoulder. "Only my ego."

He didn't understand, and said so.

"I guess I didn't tell you that Rusty died behind the wheel of a vintage convertible…with a blond starlet at his side. They'd been drinking and carousing for days. Who knows where they were headed when he lost control of the car?" She sighed. "Steering column impaled him, and the impact threw his date forty feet from the car. Last I heard, she was still in traction."

She tried to sound so matter-of-fact, so distanced, so emotionless. But she hadn't fooled him; the facts surrounding the accident had hurt her almost as much as losing Rusty. *And what makes you think* you're *the man to help her get through it?* he asked himself. Because he knew better than anyone that hadn't been the first time she'd lost someone in a car crash.

In his opinion, ol' Rusty must have been plum loco; if *Reid* had had the good fortune to marry a woman like Cammi, he sure wouldn't be chasin' skirts!

"Whirlwind romances are doomed from the start," she added in that same dull, soft-spoken voice.

Sorry to hear that, pretty lady, he thought. Because what he felt for her could be described exactly that way.

"We barely knew one another," Cammi continued. "Had absolutely *no* business getting married."

She must have loved the big idiot; why else would she have said "I do"?

"Thought I loved him," she said, as if reading his mind. He watched her pick at a nub on her place mat. "I thought wrong."

Evidently, there had been enough of *something* between them to make her believe she could start a family with the guy.

She looked up to say "Only good thing to come of that marriage was the baby." Cammi stared into space, blinking. "And now…"

And now she didn't even have that. Seeing her so sad, on the verge of tears, made his heart ache, made him want to bundle her up in a big hug and apologize for asking about What's His Name.

Definitely time to change the subject. He searched his mind for something upbeat to talk about. No one was more surprised than Reid when he said, "My timing couldn't be worse, considering the circumstances, but I don't want to let you slip away. So when you're ready…" Now that he'd started, he couldn't very well back out of this. Well, he *could,* but then he'd never know if she felt the same way. If maybe someday she *might* feel the same way. "…I was wonderin' if we could get to know one another better."

Feeling like a stuttering, blithering idiot, Reid clamped his jaws together. He got up, walked around to her side of the table, took her hands in his and stood her up. Oh, but she felt good in his arms! So good, he regretted not having done it sooner. A *lot* sooner. Cammi all but melted against him. Could it mean that, despite all she'd said about whirlwind romances being doomed, she felt the same way? *Well, a guy can hope.*

"You're something else," he said again.

She'd wrapped her arms around him, almost automatically, he noticed, pressing her dimpled cheek into his shirt. Now Cammi looked up, stared into his eyes. He could see that what he'd said had confused her. She looked over his shoulder, as if her response was written on the wall behind him. Her voice trembled when she said, "Reid, I—"

Fingertips to her lips, he shushed her. He didn't want to hear anything logical right now. Didn't want to hear that it was too soon after Rusty's death, too soon after the miscarriage, too soon after they'd met. Just because her reasons made sense didn't mean he had to like them!

"What's past is past," he said. And cradling her lovely face in his hands, he kissed the tip of her nose, her forehead, her chin, wishing with each kiss he could erase her every worry and doubt, her grief and sorrow. "I'm sorry as I can be that you lost your baby, but I want you to know that even if you hadn't, it wouldn't have mattered to me. I would gladly have helped you raise that young'un." Though he hadn't consciously given the matter any thought, Reid meant every word.

The look on her face told him Cammi thought that when she'd opened those French doors she'd let a crazy man inside. And he couldn't very well deny it, because he *was* crazy…crazy about her!

He'd never experienced anything like this in his life. Maybe he ought to take things easy, slow down, find out if this was an infatuation or the genuine article.

One look into her lovely face erased all doubt. He was pushin' thirty, and falling in love for the very first time! He pulled her closer, lifted her face and kissed her. He'd held plenty of women this way, kissed them, but never had he felt like *this*. His brain must have short-circuited, because he didn't know if he liked the wacky thoughts tumbling in his head, in his heart...or hated them. He thought he'd survived every "first time" experience a man could have, but this? Not even as a teenager had he felt so out of control.

He took a step back, hoping to get some perspective, hoping Cammi wouldn't notice that her kiss had left him as breathless as a moony-eyed boy. But one look into her gorgeous face added another first to his list: Always before, *Reid* had been the protector, the nurturer in his relationships. This time, he felt safe, knowing Cammi would look out for him as fiercely as a mama lion watches over her cubs. His heart, his feelings, his needs would always be safe in her care— somehow, Cammi sensed that she was the reason he felt unguarded and helpless in the first place!

At rodeo-sponsored charity auctions, bids for a date with Reid outdid the others. He'd been voted Rodeo Bachelor of the Year three times over. His cowboy cronies good-naturedly named him "The Filly Magnet." And thanks to his talent for smooth-talking, women he'd romanced dubbed him "Slick." Reid almost chuckled aloud at the irony, because he couldn't recall a single one of those carefully rehearsed "lines" when he was with Cammi.

Maybe that's because he knew that with her, he could have things some men take for granted—home and hearth, complete with a wife, a couple of kids, a loyal family dog. He'd think of a better name than Obnoxious, but the picture would be just as pretty.

Before Cammi, he'd known there'd come a day when he'd return to the rodeo, despite his shoulder injury, even if it meant permanently disabling himself…or worse. Because what *else* was he to do with his life?

He had an answer to that question now, thanks to Cammi.

Reid tucked her hair behind her ears, stroked the pads of his thumbs across her cheeks. "Good to see some pink in your face again."

He thought she looked cute as all get-out, blushing that way. Suddenly overcome with emotion, he clutched her to him. What would it take, he wondered, to make her his own? Whatever it was, he'd do it!

But first things first. He had to 'fess up, tell her everything—that it had been *him* behind the wheel of the other car on that dreadful night. The sooner she knew the truth about him, the better.

He held her at arm's length, hoping with every breath that she wouldn't hate him. "Cammi, there's something you need to know about me. I—"

Creaking from above interrupted him, and he looked at the ceiling.

"Dad's room," she explained. "I can hardly believe he's still up." Biting her lower lip and wincing slightly, she backpedaled to open the door. "Maybe you'd better go. He'll be furious if he finds you here at this hour."

He wondered what she'd say if he told her that her dad already had plenty of reason to raise the roof if he found Reid here, and not just because of the time. In Lamont's book, Reid surmised, there would never be a good time to find Reid in his kitchen, alone with his daughter.

On a brighter note, the disruption bought him one more day before he'd have to come clean, before he'd have to deal with her reaction to the news. One more chance to show her his good side, to try to win her over.

Reid reached out, snagged her slender wrist and pulled her to him. He pressed his mouth to hers, putting everything he had into the kiss, because it had to say everything he couldn't. "I've been dreaming of finding a girl like you most of my adult life."

His words had touched her, as evidenced by her blushing smile and the bashful tilt of her head. She bit her lower lip, then whispered a shy "Good night, Reid."

Walking away from her was perhaps the hardest thing he'd ever done. From the top step of the porch, he said, "Lock up tight after I leave, y'hear?"

Cammi nodded. "And you drive safely."

Two long strides put him back inside, where he drew her close yet again. "One more for the road," he said, kissing her. "I'll call you tomorrow," he added when the delicious moment ended.

He winced when she closed and bolted the door, because a little part of him hoped she'd throw herself into his arms, tell him to stay. "You've been eavesdropping on too many of Martina's chick flicks," he told himself, descending the porch steps.

A black-and-white long-haired dog bounded up to him just then. "My guess is, you're Obnoxious," Reid said, crouching to tousle the animal's fur. "Do you know how lucky you are, living under the same roof with a gal as wonderful as Cammi?"

Obnoxious answered with a bark, then disappeared around the corner of the house. When the kitchen light went out, Reid stood and put his hands in his pockets. "G'night, pretty lady," he said. "Sweet dreams...."

The steady *clop-clop* of Lamont's cowboy boots on the hardwood floor announced his entrance. Obnoxious left the warmth of Cammi's arms, climbed off the couch and trotted up to his master, oblivious of the man's messy hair or the sheet wrinkles crisscrossing his left cheek. Lamont bent to ruffle the dog's fur.

"I thought I heard voices," Lamont told Cammi. He stood and snugged the belt of his buffalo plaid robe.

Cammi considered evading the question, but decided against it. "The man I crashed into—the one who took me to the hospital...?" She swallowed, not knowing what to make of his deepening frown. "He stopped by to see if I was all right."

Lamont didn't move, but narrowed his eyes. "At this hour? That boy never did have a lick of sense!"

"He didn't want to wake everyone by calling, so—"

"Fool. He should've waited till morning." His mouth formed a thin, taut line. "Then I coulda poked a finger into his chest, made sure he got the message loud and clear when I told him to take a hike."

Maybe Reid had been right, maybe she *was* cranky, because her dad's unreasonable attitude grated on her nerves. "What do you have against cowboys all of a sudden?" She posed the question in the most respectful voice she could muster, but just in case she missed the mark, she smiled—as camouflage. "*You're* a cowboy, let's not forget."

"True enough." He crossed both arms over his chest as Obnoxious sat beside him. "But *this* cowboy never killed anybody."

She sat up straighter.

"You heard me."

Smoothing the bangs back from her face, Cammi shook her head.

He stomped across the room and flopped onto the seat of his recliner, and the dog joined him. "I don't have anything against cowboys. It's just one in particular I don't cotton to. The boy did a good deed, driving you to the E.R., staying with you till I got there. I'll give him that. So we'll send him a box of cigars, some beef jerky, apples for his horse. Doesn't matter *what,* long as we show our appreciation." He aimed his pointer finger at Cammi. "When you get the last of this accident mess cleaned up, you'll be done with him, once and for all."

Done with him? Dad had issued an order, no question about it. Cammi was about to start listing Reid's better qualities when her father said, "Reid Alexander is the polecat who killed your mother."

Cammi couldn't admit that she'd already figured that out. Lamont had always been big on family loyalty; he'd see her defense of Reid as a betrayal.

"*He* was the lowlife who was driving the other car that night."

"Why didn't you ever tell me this before?" Cammi responded.

Scowling, he shook his head. "Didn't want to say his name, for one thing. Didn't want you girls havin' to deal with more facts than necessary. It was hard enough on the lot of you, just grappling with…" Sighing, he ended with a flick of his hand.

"But half a dozen eyewitnesses said Mom ran the red light, said it wasn't Reid's fault. I overheard at the funeral that the other driver had been cleared of all charges, right there on the scene."

Lamont only shook his head. "I don't care *what* the law said. That fool boy had no more business being out in weather like that than your mother did. What kind of parents let a fourteen-year-old boy drive, anyway?"

"I went to school with a boy who had special permission to drive at fourteen because his father was an invalid. Maybe something similar happened to Reid."

But wait…hadn't Reid called Billy his father figure? Hadn't he said that Martina had been more a mom to him than his own mother had? Cammi wondered what had happened to his mom and dad. Why had this kindly couple stepped in to parent him?

Then something dawned on her. "Driving without a license is against the law, so he would have been issued a ticket for *that* the night of Mom's accident, right?"

Lamont waved the question away. "His mama and her drunken bum of a husband were working as hired hands at the Rockin' C in those days. 'Bout that time,

Billy took a spill from the barn loft, busted up his leg pretty bad. The sheriff had taken the stepfather's license away for drunk driving. So Billy arranged for the kid to get one of those 'special permission' licenses you talked about, paid him to run into town for supplies and whatnot. Way I hear it, he was on his way to the pharmacy, to pick up Billy's painkillers, when…''

Cammi realized now what Reid had been trying to tell her earlier, when the squeaking from the floor above warned them her father could thunder down the stairs at any minute. She folded her hands. ''If he was driving legally and the accident wasn't his fault, then why do you hold Reid respon—''

''Because for starters,'' he interrupted, ''he had no business being in that king-size pickup. And because no boy of fourteen has the horse sense or the coordination to react to a situation like that. 'Specially not in the middle of a wicked storm.''

Lamont got to his feet, clomped across the floor and stopped in the doorway, the dog close on his heels. ''Get some sleep, Cammi. You need your rest.'' He hesitated, then added, ''And get any fool notions of starting up with that fella out of your mind!''

She didn't disagree. Didn't agree, either. Cammi would wait until she was back on her feet to talk this out with Reid, face-to-face. Only then would she decide whether or not to ''start up with that fella.'' ''G'night, Dad,'' she said.

''See you in the morning. Patti will be here tomorrow, so brew up an appetite.''

Food was the last thing on her mind right now. But

Cammi smiled and nodded. "It's been a long time since I had one of her big country breakfasts."

"Violet and Ivy will be here the day after tomorrow. Sort of a welcome-home dinner."

It had been a long time since she'd spent time with her sisters. Too long. "I can't wait to see them," she said, meaning it.

"Sorry if I seemed a mite gruff."

Grinning, she quoted Reid. *"Seemed?"*

Chuckling, Lamont threw her a kiss and headed upstairs, Obnoxious close on his heels.

Cammi turned out the light and snuggled under the covers, wondering how long before he sent the dog packing. Wondering if the dog would cuddle up with her again, or beg to be let outside.

Wondering how she was going to broach the subject of her mother's death next time she talked to Reid....

Chapter Seven

The doorbell rang at precisely eleven o'clock the next day. It was too late to be the mailman and too early to be the pizza guy Lily often called at lunchtime. Thankfully, Cammi had showered and changed into a white sweatsuit and sneakers, because at least she wouldn't have to explain being in a robe and slippers at this hour of the morning.

Cammi peered out the etched-glass window beside the front door and immediately recognized the lady who'd come calling. "Martina!" she said, smiling as she threw open the door.

"Good to see you, Cammi."

Martina balanced a plate of cookies in one hand, a potted plant in the other, as Cammi wrapped her in a warm hug.

Draping an arm across the woman's slender shoulders, Cammi led her into the foyer and closed the door. "Goodness, what's it been—two years since I've seen you? What brings you out this way?"

Martina stood near the staircase, dark eyes sparkling in the sunlight that filtered in through the windows. "I'm on my way back from town. Had to pick up some medicine for Billy—"

Gently, Cammi ushered her toward the kitchen. "I heard about his illness," she said. And seeing the sadness on the older woman's face, Cammi took her elbow. "Let's get caught up over coffee and cookies."

In the kitchen, Martina held out the English ivy plant. "Brought you this," she said. "It's a cutting from one I've had since before Billy and I were married."

"It's beautiful." Cammi put it on the kitchen windowsill. "Perfect," she said, standing back to admire the way sunshine gleamed from the deep green leaves.

"It was the least I could do after Reid told me what happened to you. I thought maybe it would cheer you up some."

She pursed her lips. "I don't know him well, but I think Reid sometimes talks too much."

Martina put the cookies on the table. "Baked these just this morning. I remember that your father has a weakness for chocolate chips." She took a seat at the table, watching as Cammi poured them each a cup of coffee. "You're wrong about Reid, by the way," she said, as Cammi removed the clear-plastic cover from the plate. "Usually, he's more tight-lipped than a turtle. No one was more surprised than me when he came home last night—" Martina laughed softly "—or should I say this morning, and told me where he'd been until all hours—and why."

Cammi sat across from her, slid the sugar bowl and

creamer closer to Martina. "It was quite a ways for him to come, just to see how I was holding up. Especially when he could've accomplished the same thing with a phone call."

"Not at that hour." Martina looked right, then left. "Where's Lamont?"

"He went into town, some kind of business at the bank." She paused, taking in the woman's uneasy expression. "Why?"

"Well," she said, relaxing some, "next to my Billy, Reid is the bravest man I know. I wouldn't say he's *afraid* of your dad, exactly. Let's just say whenever the name Lamont London comes up, the boy gets a tad...nervous."

Obviously, a lot more had happened on the night her mother died—and since then—than Cammi knew.

"No one blames Lamont for the way he behaved, for the things he said that night," Martina continued, "least of all Reid. We all understood that your daddy loved your mama so much, he just couldn't help himself. Grief made him do and say..." She pressed her lips together as if she couldn't bear to repeat any of it. After stirring a spoonful of sugar into her coffee, Martina added a dollop of milk. "I wasn't there, mind you, but Billy told me about it after he brought the boy home." Sighing, Martina shook her head. "Lamont was hard on Reid, mighty hard."

Cammi's heart ached, for the pain her dad had gone through that night, for the way he'd taken it out on Reid. She'd heard bits of gossip over the years, but never enough to fill in the missing pieces. And since her questions about that night were always answered with a stern "You'll have to ask your father about that,'' Cammi and her sisters had never heard the whole, unadulterated truth. ''Please, tell me what happened.''

''He called Reid a murderer—one of the kinder things he said, I might add,'' Martina began. ''He said Reid deserved to spend the rest of his days in prison for killing his Rose, for taking her from her girls, from *him*.'' A frown of disapproval creased her brow as she stirred her coffee. ''As I said, I wasn't there, and I thank God for it every time I see that worried look come across Reid's face. I'm so *glad* I didn't have to be there to hear....'' She shook her head. ''Wasn't a pretty sight, I don't imagine.''

Cammi nodded. ''Must have been awfully hard on Reid.''

''Oh, yes. Very hard.'' She sighed, looked wistful. ''He was such a happy-go-lucky boy before that night. Since then...'' She lifted her cup, blew softly across the surface of her coffee. ''Now he's an odd mix of somber and serious and devil-may-care. He looks carefree on the surface, but I know better. I know because I remember the risks he took during his rodeo days.'' Martina clucked her tongue. ''And if you had seen some of those li'l gals he dated...'' Her frown deepened and she shook her head, harder this time. ''Seemed to me he took those ridiculous awards far too seriously.''

Something told her Martina wasn't referring to rodeo buckles, earned for outlasting other cowboys on the backs of wild stallions and raging bulls. ''Awards?''

''Bachelor of the Year, for starters.'' She waved her hand as if shooing an annoying fly. ''Not one of those women could be called a lady, not in my opinion, anyway, considering how they threw themselves at him.'' Martina fanned her face with the fingertips of one hand, then slapped the tabletop. "He'd never admit it, of course, but I think he became a daredevil because he just plain didn't care whether he lived or died. I always believed he took chances hoping he *would* die in a fall.''

Cammi pictured him, Stetson at a cocky angle above his brow, western-style shirt hugging his broad chest, dusty jeans clinging to his muscular thighs as he aimed a knock-'em-dead smile at his gaggle of cloying, clinging girl groupies. Unable to explain the surge of jealous anger that pulsed through her, she helped herself to a cookie, proceeded to break it in half.

"Why did he leave the rodeo?"

"Took a nasty spill from a Brahman bull by the name of Ruthless. The fall shattered his shoulder, and the trampling tore muscles, pulled ligaments and tendons. He was at death's door, I tell you! Spent weeks in the hospital and months in physical therapy afterward. His right shoulder hasn't been the same since, which means he couldn't hold his own in competitions, not in the saddle, not with a rope." Martina leaned forward and whispered, "And every chance I get, I say a prayer for ol' Ruthless, 'cause he might just have saved Reid's hide!''

Cammi's puzzled expression prompted the woman to go on.

"See, the accidents were happening closer and closer together, each a little more serious than the

last.'' She sat back. "Only the Good Lord knows if
Reid would've survived the next one.''

The image of Reid, hobbling and helpless, made
her stomach lurch. She wondered who had taken care
of him, prepared his meals, changed his bandages,
massaged the ache from bruised muscles as he recovered. Surely not one of the floozies who'd chased after him. She took a sip of coffee, hoping to wash away
the bitter taste *that* picture had left in her mouth.

"So how's Billy?''

Immediately, Martina's bright eyes dulled with
pain and regret. "Oh, Cammi, he's not well. Not well
at all. My Billy isn't long for this old world, I'm
afraid.''

Cammi reached out, covered Martina's hands with
her own. "I'm so sorry. If there's anything I can do,
anything at all, just name it. Even if it's only to lend
an ear now and then, when things get…difficult.''

She slid one hand out, used it to pat Cammi's wrist.
"Even as a girl, you were big-hearted and sweet. Remember the time you gave your choir robe to Sally
Olsen and pretended to have laryngitis so she could
sing the solo at the Christmas service?'' Martina
grabbed a cookie and took a bite.

Ah, Cammi thought, *the good old days*…when
Martina played the organ at the Church of the Res-
urrection, and Cammi held the lofty position of being
the youth choir's soloist. She'd always believed Sally
had the prettier, better voice, and routinely said so.
But the choir master and Sally's dad had been em-
broiled in a long-standing feud…which ended the day
Cammi pretended she couldn't sing and Mr. O'Dell
gave Sally the lead.

Martina sat up straighter. "And I think you know if *you* need to talk, I'm here for you, too."

She took that to mean Reid had filled Martina in on what she'd been through since leaving Amarillo for L.A., and since returning to Texas. "Isn't it strange," she said to change the subject, "that Reid and I lived in the same town all those years, yet we never met."

"No. Not strange at all. There are miles and miles between our ranch and yours. We're in different school districts." She harrumphed softly. "Besides, Billy and I never ran in the same social circles as your mom and dad."

Cammi recalled the fancy parties her parents threw several times a year, recalled that Martina and Billy hadn't been invited to a single one. "But our families have attended the same church for as long as I can remember."

Martina shook her head. "Reid was never allowed to come to church with Billy and me. Not while his mama was married to that horrible man, anyway. He'd drink himself into a stupor every night of the week, then drag her and Reid to his church on Sunday morning." She wrinkled her nose with disgust. "It was one of those metal outbuildings on the edge of town, where the preacher spewed fire-and-brimstone sermons."

Martina leaned in to share another secret. "Folks say that man used poisonous snakes to test his followers' faith!" she whispered hoarsely, wide-eyed, one hand pressed to her chest. Martina sat back, added in a voice of disapproval, "Sadly, Reid was long gone when the cancer took his mama, and by then, he'd been nursing a grudge against the Lord for years.''

A grudge against the Lord…

Martina looked at Cammi from the corner of her eye. "You'll be good for him," she said, standing. "It's about time he settled down. I thank the Almighty that this time, he chose well. You're the answer to my prayers. Billy's, too."

It was a lot to absorb in such a short time, and Cammi didn't know how to react.

"Reid deserves some happiness." Martina pushed in her chair. "Lord knows he's had enough sorrow in his life."

Of course he deserved happiness, Cammi agreed, but what on earth made the woman think *she* could help him find it?

"Hate to eat and run," Martina said, heading back toward the foyer, "but I have to get home with that medicine. Billy had enough of it to last a few more days, but I'm not one to take chances. What if there's a storm? What if I forget to gas up the car?" She gave a nervous laugh. "Like Reverend Johnstone says, 'Trust in the Lord but lock your car!'"

Smiling, Cammi opened the front door. Giving Martina a goodbye hug, she added, "Thanks for stopping by. You've brightened my whole day. Dad's too, once he sees those cookies!"

"See you at church on Sunday?"

Cammi stiffened. Her own grudge against God made her want to shout that she had no intention of attending services, this Sunday or any other, for that matter. But out of respect to this gentle woman who'd always been devout, Cammi said, "If I'm feeling up to it, you might see me there."

"I'll pray for you," she said, squeezing Cammi's hands. "And Billy and I could use your prayers, too."

She couldn't promise to pray, but couldn't bring herself to say she wouldn't, either. So Cammi nodded and said, "Thanks again for stopping by. It was great seeing you."

"You take care of yourself, now, you hear?" And hands clasped under her chin, she said, "It's so amazing."

"What is?"

"How much you look like your mama." She laughed. "But I expect you're bored to tears, hearing what a beautiful woman Rose London was."

She'd heard it all her life, it seemed. "No, I love hearing about her."

"Well, I'll be on my way. I'll be sure to give Reid your love."

Cammi wanted to say, *No! Don't do that!* But her spunky visitor was down the steps and halfway to her car before she could form the sentence. Grinning, Cammi waved, thinking she'd like to be a speck on the wall when Martina delivered that message, because wouldn't it be interesting to see how the Bachelor of the Year reacted to *that*.

Weeks after Reid's return to Texas, Billy had met with his lawyer, and when the dark-suited man left the Rockin' C, Billy had handed Reid a legal-looking document.

"Makes perfect sense," Billy had said when Reid protested the power of attorney.

"I don't want any part of the paperwork," Martina agreed. "You're the son we never had. Surely you don't expect us to turn to strangers at a time like this."

He couldn't have refused them, even if it hadn't been "a time like this."

From that day on, Reid had taken care of all official ranch business. He made a point of discussing everything with Billy first, of course, because he sensed Billy would leave this old world easier, knowing the spread he'd spent a lifetime building was in good hands.

He'd just deposited a hefty check—money that had come from the sale of a prize-winning calf—when he heard a familiar voice behind him. Reid didn't need to turn around to know it was Lamont London, having a conversation with the next person in line. With any luck, he could duck out of the bank without being seen.

Under ordinary circumstances, he would have waited until he got outside to put on his hat and sunglasses. But no meeting with this bear of a man could be called "ordinary circumstances."

Reid strode purposefully to the door, feigning interest in the deposit slip as a way to avoid eye contact. Experience had taught him that the very sight of him brought it all back to Lamont: whose fault the accident had been didn't change the ugly fact that Rose London died that night. Rather than stirring up trouble, Reid made it a point to avoid Lamont whenever he could.

But this wasn't to be one of those times.

Lamont stepped halfway out of the teller's line.

"You're up mighty early for a fella who comes callin' in the middle of the night."

Reid had two choices: Keep walking—and appear disrespectful and guilty—or face the man.

He stopped dead in his tracks, removed his hat and shades, and looked Lamont in the eye. "Didn't want to wake the whole house by phoning. I was worried about Cammi."

Lamont's bitter chuckle echoed in the high-ceilinged, marble-floored building. "Decent man would have waited till morning."

The implication was clear. "Duly noted," Reid said, nodding.

He'd barely got his hat back on when Lamont added, "In the future, you'd be wise to avoid my spread...and my daughter."

He looked into the man's face, saw years of anger and resentment, grief and regret written in every crease. This was neither the time nor the place for an all-out confrontation, but one thing needed to be said. "Cammi's a full-grown woman, capable of making up her own mind about...things." He paused to give his words a moment to sink in. "I give you my word—I'll honor any decision she makes."

His eyes mere slits now, Lamont said, "If my girl is so much as considering spending time in your company, then she's lost her cotton-pickin' mind."

Reid stood as tall as his six-foot frame would allow and squared his shoulders. "Maybe so," he said, donning the sunglasses, "and maybe not."

He walked toward the double glass doors and stepped outside. Despite the bright sunshine, Reid felt the chill of Lamont's icy glare. If they'd been living in the days of Billy the Kid or Wyatt Earp, what he'd said to Cammi's father just now would've been dubbed ''fightin' words.'' Who was he kidding? It didn't matter that the calendar said ''Twenty-first Century''; Lamont London still lived by 1800s principles.

He'd stay away from River Valley Ranch out of respect for the man, but it would take an act of Congress to keep him from Cammi. As soon as she was able, he'd take her out for a night on the town. Afterward, he'd get her alone someplace and spill his guts, tell her the truth, that is, if Lamont hadn't spilled the beans already. If she decided it'd be too hard, living life with the man who'd killed her mother, well, it would hurt to the bone, but he'd accept it.

Behind the wheel of Billy's pickup now, he poked the key into the ignition. He sat for a moment after cranking up the truck's motor, staring straight ahead, seeing nothing. Life would be tough enough without Billy, but Reid believed he could stomach it, with Cammi by his side. Without her, though…

''Lord,'' he whispered through clenched teeth, ''if You're up there, I sure would appreciate a hand up, here.''

Reid finished up his business in town, then headed straight home. He was tempted to take the turn-off that led to Cammi's place, but the scene in the bank made him decide against it. No telling how long before Lamont returned to the ranch, and Cammi was in no condition to witness a brawl between her father and him.

About a mile before the Rockin' C drive, a shiny

black SUV with black-tinted windows barreled down the road, leaving a wake of road grit and dust in its wake. He recognized its stern-faced driver instantly. Reid knew there was nothing—not a store or restaurant, not even a gas station—between here and River Valley Ranch to bring Lamont so far out of his way.

Nothing except Reid himself, that is. Maybe, in that spirit of the Old West, Lamont had decided to call Reid out, insist on a showdown at sundown, a duel at dawn.

A foul mood descended upon him as he wondered how long he'd have to slink around, avoiding the Londons, skirting their ranch. When would they accept that he'd simply been in the wrong place at the wrong time and stop hating him for what had happened that night?

Something told him "never" answered all three questions, and his already dark mood deepened. *Quit feelin' sorry for yourself, Alexander,* he thought. *It's your own fault, after all.*

He should've listened to Billy when he tried to talk Reid out of going to the cemetery on the morning of Rose's funeral. But Reid had been certain it was the right thing to do. He'd prayed on it, he'd insisted, and he had to do what he felt the Lord wanted him to do.

Turned out the visit only made matters worse. Far worse. If he'd known what would happen when he borrowed a white shirt and tie from Billy, when he got Martina to press a sharp crease into his blue jeans, when he hitched a ride into town, then hid in the stand of pines behind Rose's grave, waiting for her family and friends to pay their last respects…

As the last mourners led the teary-eyed London

girls to a waiting black limo, Reid made his way across the velvety lawn to where Lamont stood, stiff and silent, one hand over his eyes, the other on Rose's casket.

"Mr. London?"

Slowly, he faced Reid. "What're *you* doing here?"

Back then, Lamont stood head and shoulders taller than the fourteen-year-old boy and outweighed him by fifty pounds. Still, Reid stuck by his "do the right thing" decision. Stiffening his back, he said, "There's somethin' I need to say."

Lamont went back to staring at the coffin. "Well, don't that just beat all," he said, mostly to himself. "The boy needs to say something." He cast a surly glance at Reid. "I don't care what you need. Now get yourself on home. You're foulin' the air, just by standin' there."

Reid picked at a hangnail on his thumb. Picked so hard he started it bleeding. Stuffing it into his jeans pocket, he cleared his throat. "I came here to say…I'm sorry, sir, mighty sorry about what happened the other night—"

Shoulders hunched and fists doubled up at his sides, Lamont whirled to face Reid again. "Are you deaf, boy?" His eyes all but shut in a fierce frown, he snarled, "Not just deaf, but dumb, too. Didn't I make myself clear at the hospital the other night? I pray to God I never lay eyes on you again!"

Reid took a step back and winced, prepared to take a hard right to the chin—or worse. He could have turned tail and run, but the way Reid saw it, he had a beating coming. That, and then some! Because although everyone—the police, witnesses on the scene,

doctors and nurses in the E.R., Martina and Billy—
insisted the accident hadn't been his fault, Reid hadn't
swallowed a word of it. It was Lamont's hateful
speech outside the O.R. that rang true in his young
mind: He'd killed a wife and mother. Maybe Lamont
was right—maybe there *had* been something Reid
could've done to prevent the crash. He'd likely never
know for sure, but if whalin' the tar out of Reid would
make Lamont feel better, well, he owed the man that
much.

He'd opened his eyes when Lamont said, "Don't
worry, boy. I won't sully myself by layin' a hand on
the likes of *you*."

It had taken quite a while to figure out what that
meant. Even now, the knowledge created a hard knot
in Reid's gut. It would have done his conscience a
world of good if Lamont *had* thrashed him back then
in the graveyard.

He steered the pickup into the Rockin' C drive,
parked it beside the detached garage and stomped into
the house, where Martina stood at the stove, stirring
something in a deep pot. "What was Lamont London
doing here?" he asked, hanging his jacket on the wall
peg.

She sighed. "Looking for you."

"Me?"

She nodded somberly. "You, and answers. Why
you paid his daughter a call last night, what kind of
relationship you have with her, what your intentions
are—"

"Who'd he talk to, you or Billy?"

"Billy, mostly."

Reid grit his teeth. Billy was in no shape to be dealing with that man. "If he riled him, I'll—"

She sent him a confident smile. "If anyone got riled, it was Lamont." She went back to stirring the contents of her pot. "I'm afraid he didn't get what he came for."

"What *did* he come for, if not answers to his questions?"

Martina laid the ladle in a bright rooster-shaped spoon rest. "To lay down the law, to deliver a list of do's and don'ts to you." Grinning, she winked. "But Billy set him straight."

The scent of spicy tomato sauce wafted in the air, and she closed her eyes to inhale a whiff. "Mmm. I haven't made spaghetti sauce in ages. Lunch'll be ready in half an hour or so," she announced, sliding another pot from the cabinet. "You have plenty of time to get cleaned up." The noodle kettle sat in the sink basin under the tap water. Martina stuck her forefinger into the hissing stream and added, "Time for a quick nap, even." She shot a maternal glance over her shoulder. "I imagine you could use one, seeing as how you didn't get much sleep last night."

"I'm wide awake," he admitted. Running into Lamont at the bank, seeing him again on the road, learning he'd been here, had jarred Reid enough that he'd probably have trouble falling asleep even hours from now.

After supper that evening, Reid put Billy to bed, then helped Martina with the dishes. When the last pot was dried and put away, she kissed him good-night. "Don't stay up too long," she said, mussing his hair.

"Don't worry, I'm just gonna watch the TV news for a spell, then I'll come up." At the foot of the stairs, he wished her sweet dreams and headed for the family room.

The telephone on the end table beckoned him. He lifted the receiver, then glanced at the clock. Only nine, he thought. Too late to call her?

Only one way to find out...

He dialed her number, holding his breath, hoping she'd answer, or that her youngest sister would pick up.

"Lamont London."

He gave a sigh of frustration. "Reid Alexander," he said matter-of-factly. "I'd like to talk to Cammi."

There was a long pause before Lamont said, "I need to talk to you, Alexander. Can you meet me at Georgia's Diner?"

"When?"

"Now."

Reid swallowed. "I reckon I can be there in half an hour."

"Fine."

Reid stared at the buzzing earpiece, wondering what Lamont London wanted with him. Well, he'd find out soon enough, wouldn't he? Reid dashed off a note and propped it against the salt and pepper shakers in Martina's spotless kitchen. *"Went to Georgia's for a confab with Lamont London,"* he wrote. *"If I'm not back by morning, send in the S.W.A.T. team."* And he signed it, *"Love, Reid."*

He drove slightly more than the speed limit, hoping

to establish some kind of home-turf advantage by arriving first. Unfortunately, Lamont must have had the same notion, for when Reid pulled into the parking lot, he saw the man, backside leaning against the fender of the enormous black SUV, arms folded over his chest and gray Stetson riding low on his forehead. The instant he saw Reid, he uncrossed his booted ankles and stood, feet shoulder-width apart.

"Evenin'," Reid said, walking toward him.

Lamont gave a halfhearted salute and one nod of his head. "Evenin'." He started for the diner's entrance. "Thanks for agreeing to meet me."

"No problem," Reid said, opening the door. He stood aside as the older man entered. "You made good time getting here."

Lamont removed his hat. "There wasn't any traffic." He led the way to a table in the rear of the restaurant and pulled out a chair. "Coffee?" he asked when the waitress came over.

Reid nodded at the girl. "No cream, no sugar."

"Ditto," Lamont agreed.

She scribbled on her pad and left them alone with their frowns. A minute of complete silence passed before she delivered the coffee and moved on to take another order.

Lamont spoke first. "Guess you're wondering why I asked you to meet me here."

Reid began making an accordion out of a paper napkin. "You could say that."

"About…the accident…" Lamont cleared his throat, coughed into a weathered fist. "Just wanted to say…maybe I was a mite hard on you back then."

Lamont was a proud, stubborn man. This apology

hadn't come easy. Reid saw no point dragging things out, making him grovel. "I'd have done the same in your shoes," he admitted. "Or worse."

Lamont met Reid's eyes, held his gaze for what seemed an eternity before saying, "I'll admit, it still doesn't set well—your courtin' my girl, that is."

Courting. Reid took a long, slow sip of his coffee, thinking Lamont would have fit in real well back in the Wild, Wild West days. "I wouldn't worry too awful much about me courtin' Cammi if I were you." He unfolded, then refolded the paper accordion. "I haven't told her yet that it was me behind the wheel of that truck." Reid took a deep breath, exhaled. "She'll likely send me packing when she finds out."

A strange expression darkened Lamont's face, and it puzzled Reid.

"I just wanted to clear the air in case..." Lamont winced. "I want Cammi to be happy, is what I'm tryin' to say."

"She's been through a lot lately," Reid agreed. He shook his head. "I know it sounds squirrelly, me talkin' this way so soon after meeting her, but I'm crazy about that girl of yours. If she'll have me, if she can find it in her heart to forgive me for..." Reid didn't think he needed to spell out why, not to Lamont of all people. "If she'll have me," he said again, "I swear, I'll do right by her."

Lamont drained his mug, put it back onto the table with a *thud*. He tipped it this way and that, watching the remaining drops of coffee swirl around in the bottom of the cup before saying, "Then I reckon as long as we're in agreement on that, you 'n' me don't need to be best friends, now, do we?"

"No. I reckon we don't."

So they'd come to an understanding. Cammi's happiness was more important than what either of them wanted. Lamont had as much as agreed to give his blessing—*if* his daughter wanted Reid. *Mighty big. "if,"* he said to himself.

"Well, guess that about says it all," Lamont said, standing. He unceremoniously threw a five-dollar bill on the table and pressed the Stetson into place on his head, then extended his right hand. "I don't know if I would have come here, in your shoes, so thanks for meeting me."

Reid gave his meaty hand one hearty shake. "No, sir," he said. "Thank *you.*"

Lamont's brows knitted in the center of his forehead. "Thank me? For what?"

Releasing his hand, Reid said, "Let's just say if I'm ever lucky enough to have young'uns of my own, I hope I can love 'em as unselfishly as you love yours."

Drawing his head back slightly, Lamont blinked several times. "Well, I…uh, well—"

The shadow cast by Lamont's hat brim made it impossible to know for sure, but Reid had a feeling the man was blushing. "Guess we oughta be hittin' the road," he said, saving him. "Sunup comes mighty early, and Billy's new ranch hands haven't learned the ropes yet."

This time Lamont held the diner door open. "He didn't look so hot when I saw him today," he said as Reid passed by.

"The docs figure he has six months, tops."

The men walked side by side to Lamont's truck. "That's a sorry shame. I always liked old Billy...."

"Can't think of a soul who doesn't."

Again, Lamont nodded. Then he opened his driver's door and climbed into the SUV's cab. "Be seein' you," he said, slamming the door.

Reid answered with a two-fingered salute to his hat brim. *Yeah,* he thought, *I reckon you will.*

At least, he hoped so.

It depended entirely on how Cammi would take it when he told her...everything.

Chapter Eight

Dinner the following night with the family was everything Cammi expected it to be—and then some.

For every delicious morsel of food Lamont's housekeeper served up, Violet and Ivy dished out unwanted advice. Like blond stereo speakers, the twins voiced shock that their eldest sister had secretly married a near stranger, had been carrying his child when he died. They were harsh and disappointed that Cammi had kept her hardships to herself these past few months.

Lily, usually the most likely to take up for the underdog, didn't participate in the heated discussion. She sat, sullenly poking at her food, too preoccupied to join either side of the debate. Cammi made a mental note to seek her out later, find out what had caused the uncharacteristically gloomy mood. Hopefully, nothing had happened to one of Lily's beloved animals.

Lamont finally put an end to the twins' carping

criticisms. "Give it a rest, girls," he scolded, throwing down his napkin. "I thought we put this kind of squabbling behind when you left kindergarten."

He meant well, Cammi knew. And the Good Lord knew the man deserved one peaceful meal, after all she'd put him through these past few days…these past few *years*. But he had no idea that his fatherly refereeing always caused more harm than good; inevitably, it widened the gap separating Cammi from Violet and Ivy.

As if to prove her theory, the twins traded "I told you so" glances, a silent signal that Cammi read to mean, *the prodigal returneth*. She loved her sisters dearly, but at times like these, it was very difficult to *like* them.

Maybe if she could steer them away from her mistakes…

"So, how's the boutique, Ivy?" The shop had been Ivy's lifeblood ever since her fiancé left her at the altar.

The youngest twin's blue eyes brightened. "Wonderful!" she said smiling. "I'm expecting a shipment of turquoise jewelry. You'll have to stop by and pick out a pair of earrings—my welcome-home gift to you."

Cammi patted Ivy's hand. "You're a peach, kiddo." And turning to Vi, she said, "And the dance studio? How goes it?"

"Oh, it's tap-tap-tapping along." Vi gave a proud smile. "I have nearly two hundred students this year."

"I'm so proud of you, Vi! Any shows on the calendar?"

She nodded enthusiastically. "I'll get you tickets. You'll love the Thanksgiving performance. We're dancing to numbers from *Phantom.*"

Cammi thought Vi spent entirely too much time at her school, but who was she to talk when she'd just blown two whole years trying to make it as an actress. As for Vi's love life, well, Cammi knew better than to bring *that* up. She couldn't think of a single boy Vi had brought home who hadn't riled Lamont. But then, in all fairness to Vi, she couldn't name a guy *any* of them had brought home that he'd approved of.

And Reid Alexander would prove to be the source of his biggest disapproval yet. Which was a shame, because she sensed that beneath Reid's ladies' man facade lived a good old-fashioned hero. Cammi remembered the soft warmth of his lips, the steady beat of his heart against her as he tenderly wrapped her in his muscular arms. She wondered what it might have been like if Lamont didn't already know Reid's history. "Dad," she'd say, striking a game-show hostess pose, *"this is Reid, the fella who killed Mom...."*

Immediately, what started out as a halfhearted joke backfired. For the thousandth time, she pictured that life-altering night, when lightning crackled, slicing through the storm-black sky. She imagined rain, sheeting over the horribly misshapen station wagon, where inside her mother lay bleeding and helpless and—

"Good grief, Cammi," Lily said, her brow furrowed with concern, "you're pale as a ghost. Why don't you go into the den and stretch out on the couch for a while? Ivy and Vi will help me with the dishes."

The twins exchanged another secret glance, making

Cammi wish that just once, she shared their talent for each knowing what the other was thinking.

For the past half hour, Cammi had been trying to ignore the fact that she'd been feeling light-headed. No surprise, really, considering that only a few days ago—

"She's right," Lamont agreed, mistaking Cammi's hesitation for reluctance to do as Lily suggested. "Take a nap or something while we clean things up in here." He smiled at Lily, then at Vi and Ivy in turn, his not-so-veiled hint inspiring them to nod their agreement. They reminded Cammi of those doggies people liked to perch in the rear windows of their cars.

"I just hate to miss out on dessert," she teased, standing on wobbly legs.

"We promise to save you a slice of pie," Lily said, reaching out to steady her. "Now, get on out of here. How do you expect us to bad-mouth you behind your back if you're right here facing us!"

Laughing, Cammi held up her hands in mock surrender. "All right. I give up." She headed for the family room, grateful to have a family who loved and cared about her despite the stupid mistakes she'd made. A dizzy spell stopped her halfway down the hall, and Cammi grabbed the wall's chair rail for support.

"I'm really worried about her, Dad," she heard Lily whisper. "How much blood did she lose, anyway!"

"I don't know" was his answer. "I wasn't there."

"You weren't?" That voice belonged to Vi,

Cammi realized. "If you weren't there, how'd she get to the hospital?"

Lily said, "The guy she crashed into the other night drove her."

"Crash!" said Ivy. "What crash?"

Cammi heard Lily's impatient sigh. "Do you *ever* hear a word anyone says," she droned, "if it isn't about *you?* I told you on the phone—Cammi had an accident coming into town, and she met up with the other driver the very next day. Started having her miscarriage right before his very eyes, and he drove her to the E.R."

"If he hadn't been there for her," Lamont put in, "God only knows what might have happened to Cammi."

She'd had the same thought, dozens of times. Reid truly had saved her, in every sense of the word. But she never would have guessed her dad could be open-minded enough to admit it!

"So who *is* this guy?" Ivy asked. "Do I know him?"

Lily cleared her throat. "Ever hear of Reid Alexander?"

Silence, then Violet said, "Not the rodeo cowboy whose name is always in the gossip columns...."

Leave it to Vi, Cammi thought, *to point out the most negative thing about him.*

"One and the same," Lily said.

"I've seen pictures of him in all sorts of magazines and newspapers," Vi added, "and let me tell you, he's one good-lookin' dude!"

"Now, girls..." Lamont said.

Cammi recognized it as a warning to change the course of the conversation, now.

Evidently, all three of her sisters caught the admonition, too; she heard the unmistakable sounds of plates being stacked, silverware being gathered, tumblers being collected. "We'll take care of these, Dad," Ivy said. "Go on into the den and keep Cammi company. We'll all have pie in there together when the dishes are done."

Cammi heard the feet of his chair scrape across the thick Persian rug that blanketed the polished dining room hardwood. "Think I'll take you up on that offer," he said. And chuckling, he added, "I wouldn't complain if a cup of coffee came with my pie."

She craned her ears, trying to figure out what had caused the sudden, complete silence.

"How 'bout you, Cammi," Lamont called, his voice a tad louder. "Should the girls bring you a cup, too, when they deliver your pie?"

Not even as kids had his daughters been able to get anything past him. What made her think she could pull the wool over Lamont's eyes now that he'd had a decade or more to hone his parenting skills? He had her, dead to rights; no point now in pretending she'd been heading back toward the dining room from her perch on the family room couch.

"Sounds great," she muttered.

Vi sounded genuinely surprised when she said, "Dad, how'd you know Cammi was standing there?"

"My lips are sealed," he drawled.

The girls' giggling voices faded as they moved into the kitchen. Cammi waited, and when Lamont caught up to her, he grinned and slung an arm around her. "So, heard any good gossip lately?"

Red-faced and shaking her head, Cammi sighed. "Well, I guess you're a shoo-in for the Best Ears in Texas award."

He ushered her into the family room, and as she settled onto the couch, he rubbed his chin. "Best Ears award, eh?"

What he'd said about Reid echoed in her mind. "You're up for Father of the Year, too."

He slouched into his recliner. "And why's that?"

"What you said about Reid…" She shrugged. "It was a nice thing to say, that's all."

A shadow crossed his face, and the merry grin and twinkling eyes were replaced by a dour expression. Cammi would have asked what happened to change his mood…if she hadn't been so afraid of the answer.

With Lamont having turned in earlier than usual, and Lily in the barn tending her critters, Cammi had the darkened house all to herself. She slid the napkin bearing Reid's phone number from her pocket, where she'd tucked it earlier.

The mantel clock counted out the eight o'clock hour as she lifted the receiver from its cradle. Too late to call, given Billy's condition? Hopefully not, she thought, pressing the numbers.

For the next few minutes, Cammi and Martina exchanged pleasantries. Then the older woman said, "Why do I get the feeling you didn't call just to talk to me?"

Cammi heard the smile in her voice and was about to admit she'd called for Reid when Martina laughed.

"He's right in the next room, watching a baseball game with Billy. I'll get him."

Because of the ALS, Reid's time with his old friend was limited, she knew. "No, don't interrupt them," she said. "Can you have him—" She heard the phone hit a hard surface, then the *thud* of slant-heeled cowboy boots nearing the phone.

"Hey, there, pretty lady. What can I do for you?" Reid said cheerfully.

The imperious tones of the twins' voices still ringing in her ears, she needed to hear his voice. "Just wondering if you'd heard from the mechanic, is all."

"Nope. Guess that means you haven't either, right?"

"Hard to tell when we'll get our wheels back."

"*If,* y'mean," he said, chuckling. "So...where's your dad?"

"Upstairs, asleep probably."

He paused. "Think it's safe for me to stop by?"

Cammi coiled the phone cord around her forefinger, trying to come up with a legitimate reason to say yes.

"I won't stay long, I promise."

She wished Lamont hadn't confirmed her suspicions about Reid's involvement in her mother's accident. Cammi didn't know how she'd behave face-to-face with him.

"There's something I have to tell you, and..."

He's said as much last night, in the same dreary tone of voice. Cammi realized Reid wanted her to hear from *him* that he'd been driving the other car that night. "And what?" she urged.

"...and something I need to ask you."

She couldn't imagine what he might want to ask her. But last night, while tossing and turning on the pillowy leather sofa in Lamont's den, Cammi had made a decision, and Reid had a right to know what conclusions she'd come to.

"Okay," she said. "But park at the back end of the drive, and I'll meet you in the barn."

"No way! You're supposed to stay off your feet, remember?"

"It's just a short walk from the house, and I'll take it easy. Once I'm out there, I'll put my feet up on a hay bale or something, I promise."

"I dunno. Goes against my better judgment. Maybe I should wait until—"

"I hate to sound cranky," she interrupted, reminding him what he'd said last night, "but it isn't your call."

Another pause, then he said, "I don't think you're strong enough yet."

"Let me be the judge of that, will you?" When he didn't respond, she added, "We'll have more privacy out there than in the house."

After a moment, Reid said, "Look, what I have to say can wait until you're on your feet. It's nothing urgent, nothing that's worth putting your health in jeopar—"

"Don't patronize me, Reid. I know my own limits."

He heaved a heavy sigh. "Anybody ever tell you you're mule-headed?"

She heard the teasing in his voice. "Oh, I've been told so a time or two."

"Yeah, well, I can be stubborn, too, y'know."

Which meant he could simply refuse to come over. Disappointment nagged at her, compelled her to say, "So you don't want to see me, then."

Another sigh. "Aw, Cammi, you disappoint me."

"Why?"

"I never figured you for someone who'd fight dirty."

"Curiosity killed the cat, they say."

"Okay, I give up. What does *that* mean?"

"I'm itching to find out what you want to tell me. And what you want to ask me. The sooner I find out, the sooner I'll be able to relax!"

"Stubborn," he said, chuckling, "and tricky, too."

"See you in half an hour!" Fifteen minutes later, Cammi went searching for a tablet and pen. Finding them in the end table drawer beside her father's recliner, she wrote, *"Dad—back soon. I'm visiting with Lily. Don't worry, I'm being careful. Love, Cammi."* There was a roll of cellophane tape in the drawer, too. Snapping off a piece, she used it to secure the note to his recliner's headrest.

Flinging an afghan over one shoulder, she carefully and quietly unlocked the French doors and tiptoed across the deck. If she took it easy, as she'd promised Reid, the two-minute hike from the house to the barn would be a cakewalk.

And it would have been, too…if the moon hadn't slid behind a cloud, darkening the path, causing her to catch the toe of her sneaker on a tree root.

Twenty-five minutes into the ride, it was all Reid could do to keep from stomping on the gas and speeding the whole way to River Valley Ranch. Because the sooner he got there, the sooner he could lay his cards on the table.

"And the sooner she can boot you out the door," he said to himself.

Twin lights up ahead caught his attention. Reid recognized them as the lampposts perched atop flagstone columns flanking River Valley's entrance. He passed between scalloped wrought-iron gates and coasted down the long asphalt drive ribboning from the highway to the ranch house. Though he'd seen it half a dozen times, it was hard not to be awestruck by the enormous structure. It seemed oddly out of character for a man like Lamont—hard, intimidating, and stern—to design and build a place so welcoming, right down to the many-paned windows that glowed with warm amber light. So out of sync, in fact, that Reid wondered how involved Rose had been in creating the architectural plan.

Reid didn't turn onto the wide wooden bridge that would lead him to the semicircular drive, but followed the gravel cutoff instead, and parked the pickup beside the massive red barn, just as Cammi had asked him to do. Not even the thick cloak of darkness could hide its perfection. Lamont didn't do anything halfway, as evidenced by the perfectly plumb doors to the crisp-edged white trim.

Leaving Billy's keys in the ignition, he eased the driver's door shut and headed toward the outbuilding. He half expected Cammi to be outside, waiting for him, but breathed a sigh of relief that she wasn't; she needed her rest if she hoped to recuperate quickly.

Reid knocked softly on the door, then pulled it open. *"Pssst,"* he whispered, "Cammi..."

"Nobody in here but us chickens."

He didn't recognize the voice, but remembered Cammi saying that her sister spent more time in the barn than in the house. As he tried to recall her name, a younger, smaller version of Cammi leaned out from behind a stall door. "Can I help you?"

"You must be Lily," he said, smiling as he walked toward her.

Grinning as if she'd just run into an old chum, she met him halfway. "And you must be Reid," she said, extending a hand.

Like Cammi, Lily had a firm, no-nonsense grasp.

"If you're looking for my big sister, she isn't here."

Puzzled, he said, "She told me to meet her here in half an hour."

Lily's brow furrowed. "How long ago was that?"

He glanced at his wristwatch. "Little over half an hour ago."

Her frown deepened. "Isn't like her not to follow through. Not like her to be late, either." Suddenly, she bolted to the door.

Her fear was contagious; since Reid had longer, stronger legs, he passed her without even trying.

"She would've followed that path," Lily called from behind. "The one just to your left, there."

Silhouetted by the back porch light, Cammi lay curled on her side next to the walk. "Cammi…" he said, getting down on one knee. Cradling her close, he stroked her hair. "Aw, Cammi, what have you gone and done to yourself this time?"

She lifted a hand to her forehead, wincing when she smoothed back the bangs. "Clumsy me," she said, a half smile on her face. "Caught my toe on a tree root."

Lily ran up and knelt beside them. "What happened, Cammi? Are you crazy? What're you doing out here? You're supposed to be resting." She cringed at the sight of the bruised lump on her sister's forehead. "Oh, would you look at *that!*" She met Reid's eyes. "You think it's a concussion?" Focusing on Cammi, she added, "You okay? Should we call 911?"

Cammi's giggles started slow and quiet, escalating to a hearty laugh. "Easy, kiddo," she said, breathless, "I'm fine. Just got the wind knocked out of me, that's all."

"Let's get you into the house," Reid said, picking her up.

Cammi slipped her arms around his neck, rested a cheek on his shoulder. "I can make it under my own steam, you know."

He pressed a kiss to her temple. "Yeah, I'm sure you can. But humor me, will ya?" He walked a few steps before saying, "You gave us quite a scare."

"Sorry."

Lily walked backward in front of them. "How long do you think she was out?"

"Hard to tell." He pressed his cheek to Cammi's. "She doesn't feel cold, so at least shock hasn't set in."

"Still, maybe we should—"

"Hello-o," Cammi teased, waving one hand. "I'm right *here.*"

"Oh, I don't know about that," Lily protested, tapping her temple. "If you were all *here,* you wouldn't be outside. Not in your condition. Especially not without telling anyone where you were going.''

''I left Dad a note in case he woke up and came downstairs for a bedtime snack.''

''Fat lot of good that would have done if…'' Lily rolled her eyes. ''You should've called the barn. Why do you think Dad had a phone installed down there?''

Reid didn't like this turn of events, and decided Cammi didn't need any more upset. ''It's mostly my fault she's out here. I should have insisted on meeting her at the house.'' He clamped his teeth together. ''Better still, should've waited till she was better.''

Cammi laid a finger over his lips, effectively silencing him. As he carried her up the back porch steps, Lily dashed around him and held the door open.

''You get her settled in the den,'' she suggested, ''and I'll get an ice pack for that nasty bump on her head.'' And when all three stepped inside, Lily closed the door. ''I think we should call someone.''

Cammi groaned. ''Who?''

''If not 911, then Doc Albert, at least.''

''No,'' Cammi said.

''We should drive you to the hospital, then.'' Lily ran alongside Reid as he carried Cammi down the hall.

''No need for that,'' Cammi insisted. ''I'm fine.''

Lily tagged Reid's heels into the den. ''But you could have a concussion!''

''Lily,'' Cammi said, as Reid gently deposited her on the sofa, ''I love you for caring, but I'm okay. Honest. Now relax, will you?''

Reid grabbed an afghan from the back of the couch,

shook it out and draped it over Cammi's legs. "She's right, Lily. Sort of."

"Sort of?"

Cammi said, "Lily, doesn't Elmer need a feeding?"

Reid laughed. "Elmer? Who's Elmer?"

Cammi cupped a hand beside her mouth and whispered, "She's playing mama cow to an orphaned calf."

"Hello-o," Lily mimicked Cammi. "I'm right *here.*"

"Elmer's the calf?" he asked.

Pocketing her hands, Lily nodded.

"Go on and feed him, then. I'll stay with Cammi."

"But…but what—"

"I've seen a couple hundred concussions in my day, thanks to the rodeo. I know the signs. First hint of anything more serious than a headache, I'll drive her to the hospital. You've got my word on it."

She mulled that over a bit. "Dad's gonna have a fit if he comes downstairs and finds you here again."

Despite their recent meeting at the diner, the idea of facing Lamont on his own turf unsettled Reid more than he cared to admit. He pictured the man's blazing gray eyes, the firm set of his chin. "I can handle him."

Lily said to Cammi. "Your boyfriend here has a great sense of humor. He thinks 'cause he rode Brahman bulls and wild stallions, he can handle Dad." She punctuated her statement with a merry giggle.

Cammi's eyes widened and her cheeks turned bright pink. "Lily, what a thing to say." She clucked her tongue. "Reid isn't my— He's not my *boy-friend*."

"Whatever you say." She giggled again. "I'll be right back with that ice," Lily added, disappearing around the corner.

Boyfriend, Reid thought, harrumphing under his breath. He'd never much cared for the term, so why had Cammi's remark stung like a cold slap?

He barely had time to form the question before Lily was back, towel-wrapped ice pack in hand. "If you need me," Lily said, handing it to Reid, "just pick up the phone and dial 55 to ring the barn."

She didn't wait for him to agree, and he didn't wait for her to leave before tenderly holding the cold pack against Cammi's bruised forehead. "Where do you keep the aspirins in this mausoleum?" he asked, grinning.

She held the ice pack in place with one hand, pointed toward the hall with the other. "Powder room, third door on your right."

He got to his feet. "Drinking glasses?"

"Kitchen, cupboard above the dishwasher."

From the hall, he said, "Any suggestions, in case I run into your dad on the way?"

Squinting one eye, she focused on the ceiling for an instant. "Run like crazy?"

Reid laughed. "You believe in the power of prayer." Thumb aiming heavenward, he said, "Have a word or two with The Big Guy for me, will ya?"

He couldn't help but notice how her eyes darkened and her smile dimmed. Made no sense, considering the state of his own soul, but it bothered Reid that she seemed to have lost faith in God. He made a mental note to talk with her about it…later.

She'd dozed off by the time he got back with aspirins and cool water to wash them down with. "Cammi," he said quietly, nudging her shoulder.

Her long-lashed eyes fluttered open, then zeroed in on him. "Hi," she said, her voice soft and sleep-husky. Levering herself up on one elbow, she held out a hand so he could give her the aspirin.

One by one, she swallowed them, then drained the glass of water. "Thanks," she said, lying back on the pillow. A slow, half smile brightened her face. "Once again, it's Reid Alexander to my rescue."

He adjusted the ice pack, then tidied her covers. When she'd called him her hero at the hospital, he'd shrugged it off. She'd only been kidding, he told himself; no point taking it seriously. He couldn't pretend she was teasing now. Not while she looked at him as if he'd hung the moon.

"You're gonna have a big ol' goose egg this time tomorrow," he said to change the subject. He couldn't afford to get too used to the idea that she thought of him that way, because as soon as he'd told his story, chances were better than fifty-fifty that she'd change her mind.

"So what's on your mind? You said you wanted to come over here to tell me something."

As if he needed the reminder!

"And that you wanted to ask me something."

Nodding, Reid shoved aside a stack of hardcover books and sat beside her on the couch. Clasping his hands together, he faced her, prepared to tell her everything. And God willing, this time he wouldn't be interrupted.

"The night we met," he began, "I kept asking myself why you looked so familiar. Wasn't until I heard your dad say his name when I called him from the hospital that I knew the answer."

She turned onto her side, crooked an arm under her pillow to raise her head slightly. No question about it, Reid told himself, he had her full attention.

He slid the battered leather wallet from his back pocket and removed the laminated obituary he'd carried for more than thirteen years.

"What is it?" she asked when he handed it to her.

"See for yourself."

Cammi sat up a little, adjusted the light so she could read it. He watched as she bit her lip, as her gorgeous eyes filled with unshed tears, heard her sharp intake of air when she got to the part that said, *"Rose London is survived by her husband of fourteen years and four young daughters."*

Her hand was shaking when she gave it back to him. "Why do you carry that with you?"

Should he tell her that, when awards and fawning women and the admiration of his rodeo pals threatened to turn him cocky, he'd take out the article and make himself read it—a reminder of just how ordinary and rife with human frailties he truly was? What better way to answer her truthfully? And so he spelled it out, leaving out just one detail.

She sat up and planted both sneakered feet on the floor. Hands folded primly in her lap, she met his eyes. "Why are you telling *me* these things?"

He took a deep breath, held it a second, then released it slowly. There was no easy way to say it, so Reid simply said it.

"Said in the obit that your mama died in a car accident, and…"

She licked her lips, eyes wider than ever.

"…and it was me behind the wheel of that other car."

Cammi looked away, focused on something on the floor, then stared up at the ceiling. "I know."

She'd whispered it, so maybe he'd heard her wrong. Reid leaned forward, heart pounding. "You *know?*"

Then, boring into his eyes with hers, she sighed, "Yes. I've known for quite a while."

He hung his head, slapped a palm to the back of his neck. "How long have you known?"

"I figured it out not long after we met. And then, Dad added more details after you left the other night."

Reid stared at her empty water glass, wishing she'd left one swallow in the bottom of it, because he didn't remember his throat ever feeling so dry, not even after hours of driving cattle over dusty fields. What did she intend to do, keep him waiting all night for her reaction? Why didn't she just point at the door, tell him to get out and be done with it already!

"I also know that it wasn't your fault."

Why did he feel there was a *but* at the end of that sentence? Dread closed in around him like thick, choking smoke, forcing him to hold his breath. If he'd been a praying man, he'd have asked the Almighty to intercede on his behalf, change her mind, open her heart.

But if he'd been a betting man, he'd have wagered there'd be no help from heaven for the likes of him....

So Reid did the only thing he could do, and told the truth. "Just don't hate me, Cammi," he said, hoping she hadn't heard the remorse and self-loathing in his voice, the guilt he'd bottled up for years. Though common sense and evidence said he had nothing to feel guilty about.

She bent forward enough to softly lay a hand on his forearm. "How could I ever hate you?"

Good question, he thought. So why did he get the feeling an answer hovered, right behind it?

Whatever made him think he had so much as half a chance with Cammi!

With other women, he hadn't given a thought to marriage. He'd watched his mother hop from man to man, each a worse life mate than the last (though she claimed every time that *"This one is my Mr. Right, Reid, honey!"*). Well, "Reid honey" had no intention of repeating her mistakes. He'd made a point of shootin' straight with his girlfriends, never promising what he couldn't deliver. When they demanded to know why he refused to make a long-term commitment, he blamed the hectic rodeo schedule, the danger of his profession...and wished them well without telling any of them the truth: If he and some li'l gal had a couple of kids together, and she wasn't the *right* li'l gal for him... *No young'un of mine is gonna live the way I did!* he had vowed.

Reid had lived by his self-imposed "flyin' solo" code for years, because it protected everyone involved from the pain and humiliation of a broken heart.

So why had he allowed himself to be vulnerable this time?

The answer was surprisingly simple: Cammi was everything he'd ever wanted in a woman, everything he'd ever dreamed of in a life partner.

Reid would never have admitted it to his cowboy cronies, but when he had trouble sleeping in one of the generic, rubber-stamped hotel rooms of the tours, he'd think of men who'd left the rodeo to spend more time with their wives and kids. On those dark and lonely nights, Reid pictured himself with a family to go home to: a tidy little bungalow with a bright red door that would bang open when he pulled into the driveway; a couple of giggling, rosy-cheeked kids who would thunder onto the porch yelling, "Look, Mama, Daddy's home!" He'd added a scene to the dream in the last few days: In the doorway, hands buried in the pockets of a ruffled apron, wearing a "for his eyes only" smile, stood their mother, his wife…Cammi.

He'd already told her how he felt he'd known her all his life, how he'd been dreaming of her for…for*ever*. Would it do more harm than good to repeat it now?

Big, silvery tears squeezed from her eyes, telling Reid she knew exactly how he felt—and that maybe she couldn't bring herself to tell him she didn't feel the same way.

It wasn't a suspicion, this knowledge that Cammi wanted to protect him from harm, from hurt; he knew it with whole-souled certainty.

Which only made him want her all the more.

With the back of her hand, Cammi dried her cheeks. "You said you had something to tell me…"

Yes, and he'd already told her.

"…and something to ask me."

He hadn't been afraid when settling onto the back of raving-mad wild stallions, had braved the wrath of enormous snorting, stomping bulls. But here he sat, adrenaline pumping and heart knocking against his ribs, too scared to ask this five-foot-two-inch slip of a thing, who couldn't weigh a hundred pounds soaking wet, to be his girl!

Clenching first one fist, then the other, Reid said, "You oughta lie back down, get some rest." He cleared his throat. "It's been a hectic couple of days."

She surprised him, getting up off the couch and settling on his lap, so much so that he nearly lost the tight control he'd been holding on his emotions. Relief coursed through him, pulsing in every fingertip, as she put her small, smooth hand into his, leaned her head on his shoulder. His arms slid automatically around her as his lips were drawn to her temple as if he'd been programmed.

"I feel like a crazy woman," she began, the fingers of her free hand playing with the hair at the nape of his neck, "for so much as considering a relationship with you." One dainty shoulder lifted in a ladylike shrug. "God help me, I am."

If a heart could sing, as the poets claimed, his was belting out a ballad now!

"But you've suffered enough," she continued, "blaming yourself for an accident that wasn't your fault. I don't want to put you through anything more.''

His singing heart went silent. All his life he'd heard the adage ''what goes around, comes around.'' Something told him he was about to be on the receiving end of the speech he'd made to women so many times. If he could trust his voice, he would tell her to spare him the gory details.

''Since I found out about…'' She shrugged again. ''Every time I see you now, I think about that night.'' She closed her eyes so tightly, the lids all but swallowed up her lashes. ''And I get these pictures.'' A tremor passed through her, shaking her from chin to ankles. Cammi stood and walked a few steps away from him, hunching her shoulders and cupping her elbows.

Didn't take a genius to figure out what she'd meant: The very sight of him made Cammi envision the accident, and because she didn't like looking at the ugly images, she didn't like looking at *him*.

Reid glanced toward the door, gave a thought or two to leaving. No, *escaping* was more like it. Because out there, he wouldn't have to look into those big, innocent eyes—eyes that saw him as the guy who killed her mother.

''No one's to blame,'' she said, finally.

But lost in his own misery, Reid had tuned her out. Much as he wanted to hit the road and never look back, he'd promised to look after her until Lily finished feeding her calf.

He glanced at the phone. If he punched the number five two times, he'd be free.

No, he'd only spend the rest of the night worrying,

because while Lily knew plenty about critters, she didn't know diddly about concussions. He'd stay and keep an eye on Cammi until he had proof that she'd be okay.

"Cammi, do me a favor."

She looked over her shoulder and sent him a small, sad smile. "Sure. Anything."

She'd agreed without hesitation, he noted, and without having a clue what he might ask of her. Heart aching, and wanting her for his own even more, Reid pulled back the afghan and patted the sofa cushion. "Lie down before you fall down, will ya?"

For just a moment, she paused, then she crossed the room and stretched out on the couch. Reid helped her settle the afghan over herself, and flopped onto the nearest chair. He waited until she closed her eyes before leaning his head against the pillowy backrest.

Then he closed his own eyes and did something he hadn't done in years.

He prayed.

Chapter Nine

Cammi woke with a start.

It took a minute to get her bearings, but a quick look around the room calmed her, for there sat Reid, fast asleep and slumped in her father's big chair, one long muscular leg outstretched, the other bent at the knee.

Cammi eased up off the couch. Gently, she draped her afghan over Reid, then sat on the edge of the sofa cushion and simply looked at him. At boots whose brown leather soles had walked the floor of many a barn and slid into hundreds of stirrups; at faded jeans that hugged calves and thighs made thick and hard by hours of heavy work. His biceps strained against the blue flannel of his snap-front western shirt, and his hands—one partially shading his eyes, the other, fingers splayed across his flat stomach—were further proof he'd given his all to every task. And those shoulders, nearly as wide as the backrest of her father's enormous chair…

Martina had said he'd injured the right one, hurt it so badly, in fact, that he'd been forced to give up rodeoing for good. If leaving L.A. had been hard on her, when she hadn't come close to "making it" out there, how much more devastating must it have been for Reid to give up a profession that had earned him awards?

Still, it seemed he'd taken it in stride. All part of his uncomplaining, take-it-on-the-chin demeanor, she acknowledged, now studying his face. Black-lashed eyes closed and a lock of raven hair falling over his forehead, he looked like an innocent boy. But Reid was more man than any she'd known, even with his angular chin resting on that damaged shoulder. It was good to see him this way—quiet and at peace, his big chest rising and falling with every soft, steady breath.

From the moment he'd stepped out of the pickup that cold rainy night, Cammi had thought he was as good-looking as any movie star. Not even his stern, no-nonsense expression could camouflage the high cheekbones, the square jaw, the strong nose and full, kissable lips.

Unconsciously, Cammi put her fingers to her own lips, remembering the way it felt when he'd pressed that very manly mouth to hers. *Swoon* wasn't a much-used word these days, but it explained perfectly how his kisses had made her feel.

She slouched, feeling more than a little defeated. In every way possible, Reid Alexander seemed perfect. *Make that perfect for me,* she thought. Because he was more than raw masculinity cloaked in plaid flannel and worn denim; somewhere deep in that barrel chest beat the heart of a good and decent man, one who'd overcome adversity and challenges and heartaches, all without turning bitter or spiteful.

Proof he was a Christian?

Once upon a time, she wouldn't have made a move without first consulting the Almighty. She'd prayed about everything, from which courses to take in school, to boyfriends, to whether or not to move to California. Well, that wasn't entirely true, Cammi admitted; she hadn't asked God's opinion about Rusty.

But shouldn't her past good behavior have counted for something? Yes, she'd messed up, stumbled, taken the wrong path a time or two. Still, didn't she have a right to think the Lord would stick by her, guide her, despite—or maybe because of—her missteps? Didn't the Good Book promise the Father would love and protect His children, *no matter what?*

"Guess not," she muttered.

"Wha-a-a?"

She crossed one leg over the other and clapped a hand over her mouth, sorry as she could be that her thoughtlessness had awakened him.

Reid stirred, wincing as he worked the kinks out of his neck and shoulders. The moment those sea-green eyes opened, they locked on her. Cammi shivered a bit under his penetrating stare. He couldn't have been asleep more than ten minutes. And she ought to know, because every fifteen minutes since Lily headed for the barn, he'd shaken her awake.

"Nice nap?" she asked, hoping the tremor that shot through her wasn't evident in her voice.

He sat up, rubbed the back of his neck, then yawned and allowed himself a full-fledged stretch.

"Not bad," he said when he finished. "How 'bout you?"

She couldn't help but grin. "Not bad," she echoed, "considering *some*one woke me every couple of minutes to shine a flashlight in my eyes."

"Sorry, but it's the only way to know for sure if—"

"I know, I know." Grinning, she waved the apology away. "You explained it every time you roused me: 'If your pupils don't dilate properly, it's a sign you might have a concussion,'" she said in the deepest voice she could muster. "I read someplace you're to check every hour, not every—"

"I read someplace that you can't be too careful," he interrupted, knuckling his eyes. When his stomach growled, he tucked in one corner of his mouth. "Sorry."

"Hungry?"

He glanced at the clock. "I shouldn't be. Hasn't been that long since I wolfed down two heaping plates of Martina's spaghetti and meatballs."

Cammi got to her feet. "How 'bout I fry us up a couple of eggs?"

He stood in front of her and, hands on her shoulders, said, "I know it'll take longer for you to show me where things are than to do it yourself, but you've *got* to start taking things easy." Reid gave her a gentle shake. "You're never gonna get back on your feet if you keep pushing yourself this way."

She liked being this close to him, liked inhaling the manly scent of fresh hay and bath soap clinging to every inch of him, liked his tough-yet-tender take-charge attitude, too. "You make me sound like a twenty-pound weakling. She reached out, played with a pearlized snap on the front of his shirt. "I'm no award-winning rodeo cowboy, but I can take care of myself pretty well, y'know."

Chuckling, he tucked her hair behind her ears. "Humor me," he said again. "How 'bout letting me take care of you—for tonight, anyway?" His stomach growled again, as if to punctuate his question.

She tidied his collar, then stepped away from him. "We'd better do *something* about that noise before my dad mistakes it for a grizzly and comes down here brandishing his trusty shotgun."

"That picture," he said, feigning a shiver, "is a nightmare in the making." He led the way to the kitchen. "Maybe you can talk him into bringing the old .12-gauge over to the Rockin' C and clearing out that nest of rattlers one of the boys found out behind the barn."

"Rattlesnakes at this time of year?"

"They love this weather we've been having."

"The rattlers aren't the only ones."

"Well, you've got an 'in' with You-Know-Who. See about getting me some protection—from snakes *and* your daddy, will ya?"

He'd asked for that favor before, in much the same way. What made him think *she* had God's ear? "Ask Him yourself," Cammi said, putting a frying pan on a front burner.

Reid opened the fridge and stuck his head inside. When he came out, an egg carton, a package of link sausages, butter and a loaf of bread were balanced in his big palms. "I've never been on very good terms with The Big Guy,'' he said, depositing the food beside the stove.

Cammi turned on the flame under the frying pan. ''And what makes you think I have?''

Reid shrugged. ''I dunno. You just seem the peaceful, contented type.''

She rolled her eyes. ''You make me sound like a cow out to pasture!''

''Hardly!'' he said, laughing. ''But seriously, you have a solid grip on reality, a way of handling the tough stuff life dishes out. I figured your faith made you that way.''

''What made *you* that way, if not faith?''

''Me?''

He laughed again, and she took it to mean he didn't feel he'd handled hardship well at all. ''You've survived a few setbacks in your life, and didn't come out too much worse for wear. How'd you cope?''

Reid took her hand and led her to the table, pulled out a chair and gently shoved her into it. ''We had a deal, remember? You'll take it easy and I'll do what it takes to keep my gut quiet.'' He grabbed a napkin from the holder on the table, flapped it open and tucked it under her chin. ''You're in for a treat, m'lady,'' he said, bowing with a flourish, ''because few people have ever experienced a four-star Reid Alexander omelette.''

He found a smaller frying pan in a low cabinet, arranged the link sausages in it and turned up the heat. Then, opening and closing cabinet doors until he found a deep-bottomed bowl, Reid added, ''I learned a few tricks under the tutelage of my second stepfather, who claimed to have been a cook in the army.''

After cracking four eggs like a master chef, he let their contents ooze into the bowl and tossed the shells into the trash can. He rooted through every drawer until he found the one holding silverware, and, holding the bowl against his chest, he beat the eggs with a fork. "For all his other faults, old Henry wasn't a half-bad teacher."

"Real good egg, eh?" she teased as he whipped the yolks and whites into a thick froth.

"Rotten egg is more like it."

There was no mistaking the ire in his voice.

"So what's your specialty—or is breakfast the only meal you can cook?"

"You haven't lived till you've eaten one of my grilled-cheese sandwiches. And I make the best boiled hot dogs on the planet."

"I see your stepfather was a practical man."

"Yeah. Practical."

"How many stepfathers did you have?"

"Four. Each one meaner and more cantankerous than the other. Thank God for Billy is all I can say." He grabbed a knife from the silverware drawer, sliced off a pat of butter and dropped it into the skillet. As it sizzled and bubbled, he tipped the pan this way and that to coat its bottom. "Your dad might not be the cuddliest codger in town, but he's rock-solid and dependable in the father department."

She heard the admiration and respect in his voice. "True. We London girls have been luckier than most."

He poured the egg mixture into the frying pan, then looked over his shoulder to say, "It's good you know it." Then, almost as an afterthought, he added, "I expect Lamont knows it, too."

As he dug around in the refrigerator's cheese drawer, she said, "We make sure he knows it, every chance we get."

Slicing off a few chunks of sharp cheddar, he nodded approvingly. "Guess he's the reason you girls are such devout Christians."

Were devout, she corrected mentally. "I can't speak for my sisters."

Reid dropped bread into the toaster and pushed the button until all four slices disappeared. He grabbed two small glasses from the drain board beside the sink and filled each with orange juice. "So you're saying you're not devout anymore?"

She didn't know what she was saying. Didn't know what difference the state of her soul made to him. "Let's just say I'm not quite as easily fooled these days as I used to be."

Once he'd set out butter knives, forks, napkins and the juice tumblers, he stirred the omelette. "That explains it, then."

She turned in the chair to see him better. "Explains what?"

"The fact that you're not as happy as you used to be."

"And this coming from a guy who's known me—what?—three days?" she said under her breath.

"Four, but who's counting," he answered, buttering the toast. He shrugged. "The night we met, there was a…" He stared off into space, the tip of his knife drawing tiny circles in the air as he searched for the right phrase. "There was a certain glow about you.

A light in your eyes. An attitude that said 'Gimme all you got, World, 'cause I can take it!'" Reid took plates from the cabinet, put two slices of toast onto each.

"Let's see you bury a husband and lose a baby in a four-month time span and come out of it grinning like a hyena." Cammi vowed never to mention either again, ever!

"Don't know if 'grinned like a hyena' describes how I took it," he said, adding eggs and sausage to each plate, "but I've seen a few loved ones planted six feet under in my day. Never even knew my daddy."

He might have been saying "pass the salt" or "what time is it?" for all the emotion in his admission.

"Ketchup?" he asked, handing her a food-laden plate.

She shook her head. "No ketchup, thanks."

"Eat up," he instructed, sitting across from her, "before it gets cold." He downed his juice in one swallow. "Nothin' worse than cold eggs."

"Funny," Cammi said, peppering her food, "but I never would've pegged *you* as a believer."

He stopped chewing and gawked at her, green eyes flashing. "I look that much like a heathen, do I?"

"Well, no. No, of course not." She felt her cheeks going hot. "It's just…well, everyone knows that rodeo cowboys have terrible reputations."

"Oh, do they, now?" He raised his eyebrows. "What kind of reputations?"

"As girl-hungry skirt-chasers. As ladies' men, as—"

He chuckled and, using his fork as a pointer, said, "Y'know what they say."

"No, but I have a feeling you're going to tell me."

"'Never judge a book by its cover.'" Using the side of his fork, he sliced a sausage, then speared it.

"So you're saying you're a Bible-thumping, Sunday-go-to-meetin', card-carrying Christian?"

His smile diminished, and the light in his eyes dimmed. "No. I'm not saying that. I honestly can't remember the last time I saw the inside of a church." He paused. "No, that's a lie. I remember it exactly: It was the day of my mother's funeral."

Cammi took a bite of toast, washed it down with a sip of juice. "How long ago did you lose her?"

He tucked in one side of his mouth and stared into his plate. "Long time ago" was his quiet reply.

"How'd you lose her?"

"Cancer."

"Sorry."

"Don't be."

"Well, looks like we have one more thing in common."

He met her eyes again. "One more thing?"

She didn't want to get into a discussion about their mutual grief. At least, not now. Maybe in a month, or in several months, after she'd had a chance to put some distance between her and Rusty, between her and the miscarriage. Maybe then she'd be able to bare her soul and revisit the subject of "us" as it related to Reid and herself.

"Better eat up," she quoted him. "Nothin' worse than cold eggs."

"One thing's worse."

She didn't know him well enough yet to interpret what that hard-edged note in his voice meant. It went against her better judgment to ask, but she did, anyway. ''What's worse?''

''A person who blames God for what's wrong with her life. 'Specially a person who loves Him with all her heart, a person who misses having Him in her life.''

On the heels of a deep breath, Cammi shook her head. ''And I suppose that 'person' would be me.''

He quirked an eyebrow. ''If the shoe fits,'' he said nonchalantly.

What riled her most was that Reid had hit the old nail square on its head. She *did* miss having the Lord to turn to, and she *did* love Him with all her heart. But how could this cowboy who seemed estranged from the Father know a thing like that?

''It's just something to chew on,'' he added, winking, ''when you're finished eating this fantastic meal, that is.''

She *would* think about everything he'd said, the very first moment she had to herself. And Cammi intended to square things with the Almighty. She smiled at him. ''You're very full of yourself, aren't you.''

And waving his fork like a white flag, Reid smiled right back. ''Don't mention it,'' he said. ''I was more'n happy to help.''

''Let's see if you still feel that way when it comes time to clean up these dishes,'' she said, giving his elbow a playful shove.

It had taken nearly half an hour after they'd cleaned up the kitchen to convince Reid he could go home.

The only reason he'd agreed was that she'd dialed the barn and asked Lily to come up to the house. Once he'd left, it took another half hour to assure her sister the danger of concussion had passed.

Now, as the first purple rays of morning began to shimmer outside the family room's French doors, Cammi continued to toss and turn, unable to put what Reid had said about God out of her mind. About the time the mantel clock struck four, she'd given up on sleep. Blaming the heavy meal for her fidgeting worked for only a little while.

Cammi knew well the reason for her restlessness, knew the way to calm it wasn't with TV or a fashion magazine.

She grabbed her mother's Bible from the bookshelf beside the fireplace and selected a verse in exactly the way her mother had taught her, letting the Good Book fall open to a random page. *"Let the Lord Jesus show you what He wants to teach you today,"* her mama would say.

Closing her eyes, her mother's well-manicured hand would guide her little girl's pointer finger, drawing circles in the air and getting closer and closer until it came to rest on a gilt-edged page. Tonight, Cammi's random selection was Isaiah 44:22.

"'I have blotted out, as a thick cloud, thy transgressions,'" Cammi whispered, "'and, as a cloud, thy sins; return to me; for I have redeemed thee.'"

Perfect, Cammi thought, smiling. It reminded her of something she'd pushed aside: that the Father understands and forgives and loves His children...even when they behave like spoiled brats. She'd made a lot of mistakes these past months. Life-altering mistakes, the biggest of which had been blaming God for the tragedies she'd suffered. None as large and grievous as feeling responsible for her mother's accident.

As a twelve year old, it made perfect sense to blame herself; as Cammi matured, common sense told her it wasn't her fault that a grown woman had put her life at risk for something as frivolous as a pretty dress, especially not a married woman with four young daughters.

Now that Cammi allowed herself to reflect on the true circumstances that led her mother to drive out into the rain that night, self-recrimination melted away. And for the first time since her mother's death, Cammi finally felt free, forgiven, blameless. It felt so good, being "right" with the Lord, that tears filled her eyes. Humbled and grateful, she bowed her head and prayed, knowing as she did that if it hadn't been for Reid's gentle persuasion, she might not have turned to the Good Book tonight.

Lord Jesus, thank You for sending a hero in cowboy boots to show me the way back Home.

Later, she'd call and thank him. Cammi snuggled into the couch and pulled the afghan over her. Reid's manly scent still clung to it, and she closed her eyes and breathed it in. The serenity it inspired was almost as reassuring as Reid's tender embrace.

Almost…

Cammi eased into drowsiness. The reservations she'd had about the right or wrong of a future with Reid faded. She had the Lord's approval, right? Why *else* would He have chosen Reid as His messenger?

*   *   *

Someday, Reid thought as he opened one eye, he'd put a muzzle on that loud-mouthed rooster. Rolling onto his back, he stared at the still-black ceiling.

He threw his legs over the side of the bed and yawned. Then, padding on bare feet across the hand-knotted braid rug, he scratched his chin, shoved the hair off his forehead, rubbed his eyes. Grabbing a towel from the cabinet under the sink, he frowned, remembering the way Cammi had sent him home.

Oh, she'd been nice enough. Reid didn't think she had it in her to be anything *but.* Smiling nervously, she'd clasped her tiny hands in front of her chest and apologized, four or five times, for behaving like a— what had she called herself?—a dim-witted little twit who didn't know her own mind.

He slid open the glass shower door just enough to reach the faucets and wiggle his fingers under the spray. Maybe he *had* met her only a few days ago, but in that time they'd spent countless hours together. Reid had learned a lot about her. She knew her mind better than anyone he could name. So all that hemming and hawing had been to spare his feelings, to salve his ego.

He stood at the window and parted the curtains. The tidy backyard was visible because of the spotlight he'd hooked up months ago so Martina could keep an eye on her rabbit hutch. The last of her summer flowers bobbed on the chilly morning breeze.

Movement off to the left caught his eye, and Reid leaned in for a better look. Steam from the shower had begun to fog the glass, so he used the outside of his fist to clear a saucer-size peephole. Before he could determine what had parted the grass in a three-inch wide swath, the window steamed up again. Quickly, he squeegeed it clean once more, thinking that no field mouse he'd ever seen could do that. Only one of God's critters could leave a trail like that, and it had fangs at one end and a rattle at the other.

Just yesterday, one of the hands said he'd found a nest of rattlesnakes in the pit that once housed the barn's old well pump.

It was rare for a rattler to hole up so near human activity, rarer still to see one stick its head outside at this time of day. Unable to survive any extremes of temperature, it had to be careful about when to hunt for food; early morning in October wasn't the warmest part of the day. Maybe a hare had scurried by—too tempting a treat to pass up, even in the chill of predawn.

Rattlers were common in this part of Texas, and Reid and Billy had exterminated their fair share of the potentially deadly snakes over the years. Soon as he'd had his shower, he'd grab the shotgun and a shovel and get rid of this bunch, too. They were a threat to the livestock and the ranch hands alike.

"What could it hurt?" Billy was asking Martina when Reid walked through the back door. She didn't have a chance to answer, because the man aimed another question, this one at Reid. "What was all the hollerin' and shootin' about, son?"

"Rattlers," Reid said evenly. "One of the new boys found a nest of 'em out back." He hung up his jacket and headed for the sink. "We got 'em taken care of," he added, washing his hands.

"Oh. Is that all. Well, good. Did you get 'em all?"

"Yeah, I believe we did. Didn't notice any of them slitherin' off, anyway."

"Well," Billy repeated, "good." Attention on his wife once more, he picked up where he'd left off: "It's warmer than usual outside. When am I going to have another chance to sit in the sunshine?"

Martina's stern expression told Reid that whatever Billy had requested didn't set well with her. "What's this crusty ol' pest want?" he asked, joining them at the table. "A day at the beach?"

Fist propped on her hip, she shook her head. "He wants me to set the chaise lounge out in the yard so he can—" she rolled her eyes "—'catch some rays.'" Shaking her head, she grinned at her husband. "Honestly. Sometimes you sound like a teenager."

The three shared a moment of lighthearted laughter before Reid promised Martina he'd set up the lawn chair, get Billy comfortable and check on him every fifteen minutes or so.

"Well," she said thoughtfully, fingertip tapping her chin, "I do have housework to do...."

Billy groaned. "If I live to be a hundred, I'll never understand you."

Neither Reid nor Martina commented, because both knew Billy wouldn't live to see his sixtieth birthday, let alone his hundredth.

"I might be shiftless right now, but I set aside some money in my day. Why don't you hire someone to do the dusting and vacuuming for you?"

"Because I'm way too finicky" was her explanation.

But Reid knew better. She'd always taken pride in

creating a cozy home for her man, and now, more than ever, she needed something to focus on besides Billy's illness, something to do other than hover over him. A dozen times in these past few months, he'd caught her standing alone in a room, eyes closed and fingertips pressed to her lips, as if praying for busywork.

Reid ended the tense moment by clapping his hands together. "So, it's all set, then. First thing after lunch, I'll dust off the old lawn chair and—"

"Why after lunch? Why not now?"

"Because, dear, impatient Billy," Martina said, patting his hand, "it'll make your day less boring that way. Besides, the sun won't be—"

Scowling, he snatched his hand back. "Don't take that tone with me, woman. I'm not totally addle-brained and helpless...*yet!*"

Martina's dark eyes widened. "I wasn't—"

"Yes, you were. Ever since we found out about this confounded death sentence, you've been walking on eggshells, treating me like I'm made of spun glass. Well, I'm tired of it, do you hear? Tired of being made to feel like a useless old—"

She ran from the room, one hand over her mouth, the other trying to keep them from seeing her tears.

Reid helped himself to a spoonful of oatmeal. "You have about as much tact as a charging rhinoceros...and I don't mean one with a credit card, either."

Billy's rasping sigh echoed in the big, country kitchen. "I know, I know. I'd slap myself in the head—if I could make my arm work.... Maybe one of you can do it for me."

Reid saw the twinkle in Billy's eye and knew the

storm had passed. "Nobody wants to slap you in the head." He winked. "Nice swift kick to the backside might be in order, though."

Billy chuckled. "Help this old fool get to his easy chair, will you, son?"

It was heartbreaking to hear the dreary note of acceptance in Billy's voice, to watch this once hale and hearty rancher wither away like Martina's summer flowers. *If God is merciful,* Reid thought yet again, lifting Billy from the chair, *He'll take Billy quick, so he won't suffer.* Because the damage ALS was doing to the man's ego was far worse than what it was doing to his body.

Sated after a hot, nourishing lunch, Billy lay back on the blue-and-white webbed aluminum chaise longue.

Within easy reach on a folding tray beside the chair, Martina had set a battery-operated radio to his favorite country-and-western station. She'd put a tall tumbler of iced tea and a plate of homemade cookies on a blue-striped dish towel, and in his lap, several favorite fishing magazines.

After covering him with an old quilt, she'd insisted he protect his head from the sun, and plopped his battered Texas Rangers baseball cap onto his balding dome. Her final touch was a pair of wraparound sunglasses she'd dug out of his pickup's glove box.

Man couldn't ask for much more, Billy thought, smiling to himself. *Well, a man could ask for a long, healthy life.* But short of a miracle, that wasn't going to happen.

He wouldn't mind the whole dying thing so much

if it didn't mean leaving Martina. Seeing as they'd never had children of their own, the idea of her being alone scared him a whole heap more than meeting his Maker. Because didn't the Good Book say that every physical ailment a man brought into Paradise would disappear in the twinkling of an eye? Or something along those lines, anyway.

After more than half a century of living the hard rancher's life, using both brain and brawn had grown routine. So routine he'd more or less taken for granted that if he wanted to heft a hay bale or add a row of numbers in the Rockin' C ledger book, he could, and with very little effort, at that. But these past few months, as the disease ate away at his pride, his dignity, his manhood, he'd learned to appreciate the smallest things, like being able to pick up a potato chip and put it into his mouth, chew it and swallow it.

Wouldn't be long, now, he knew, before Martina was forced to stick him in one of those old fogey homes, where they'd turn him into a pincushion, running tubes every which-way.

Billy sighed and shook his head. He'd made up his mind to enjoy this day as if it were his last, because according to the weather report, it might well be the final warm day of the season.

Sunshine beat down, warming him to the core, as Willie Nelson crooned in harmony with that tenor fella from the opera. Birds chirped in a nearby tree, and the quiet hum of Martina's vacuum cleaner whirred from the house—upstairs back bedroom, he guessed.

All was right with his world.

At least for now.

Thoroughly content, he closed his eyes and relaxed completely, let his arm slide off the chair until his knuckles rested among sun-warmed blades of grass. A fishing magazine slipped from the stack on his lap, but he never noticed, and it landed with a quiet *slap* beside his hand.

Billy had no way of knowing that one rattler had escaped near death this morning as Reid and the ranch hands invaded its nest. Couldn't have known it had slithered away, seeking a safe place to hide, or that later, it had decided to coil up under Billy's chair, partly shaded from the sun, yet able to bask in its warmth. How could he have known that a magazine, falling suddenly from out of nowhere, would startle the snake so badly that instinct would make it strike out…and sink its deadly fangs into Billy's hand.

Chapter Ten

Since Martina had volunteered for the first half hour of what she'd dubbed "Billy Watch," Reid went about his duties as usual.

He'd replaced a hinge on the corral gate and was about to repair the latch on one of the barn stalls when something made him stop cold, nearly stabbing the back of his hand with a Phillips screwdriver.

Sticking the tool into his back pocket, he straightened, listening for a sound that didn't belong, looking for something that seemed out of place. He heard the lowing of cows in the south field, the occasionally whinnying of stallions that trotted around the paddock. Now and then, a ranch hand's voice would call out, alerting his cohorts that the hay skid was full and it was okay to roll in another.

He stood perhaps fifty yards from where Martina had set up Billy's "sunshine event," as she called it, and from this distance, Reid could hear the strains of an old Willie Nelson hit.

Here, a bird chirp; there, a dog bark—punctuated by the quiet *bawk-bawk-bawk* of the pecking hens. Everything was as it should be—or so it appeared—so why couldn't he shake the nagging sensation that something was wrong?

Maybe it was lack of sleep, or the cold oatmeal he'd wolfed down at breakfast, or the ugly scene between Martina and Billy that made the world seem it was wobbling out of balance.

It wasn't like Billy to lose his temper that way, even more unlike him to speak harshly to Martina. But then, what man behaves normally when he knows there's a noose around his neck?

Reid couldn't dismiss the notion that the whole "Cammi thing" was causing the nagging sensations, however. If the truth be told, nothing had felt right side up since they'd met. If he needed a reason to run the other way, the list was surely long enough! Reid could neither explain nor understand why it didn't matter to him that she'd been married, that her bum of a husband made a widow of her, or that she'd lost the child conceived as a result of their union. He loved her. It was just that simple, even though he'd met her days ago, even though none of it made a lick of sense.

He chuckled to himself. Maybe the reason it felt his world had spun out of control was because it *had!*

But who was he fooling? One argument between old married people hadn't inspired this gnawing notion that something was wrong, real wrong out there. Neither had his own petty matters of the heart, for that matter. He'd lived a rancher's life long enough to trust his gut instincts, and right now, the signals were as strong as those Custer likely had sent on that fateful day. Experience had taught him if he didn't want to end up like the General, he'd better heed the warning.

Never one to panic, Reid sauntered toward the house, figuring he could look in on Billy as he checked things out. The closer he got, the more intense his belief grew that things weren't as peaceful around the Rockin' C as they seemed.

At least Billy was getting some much-needed R and R, Reid thought as he approached the lawn chair. The man hadn't budged, hadn't moved so much as an inch since Reid had started over. He was about to veer right, straight toward the house, when he realized that though he appeared to be asleep, Billy's eyes were open.

Reid covered those last steps in record time. "Billy," he said, grabbing the man's biceps. "Billy, what's wrong, man?"

Billy tried to talk, but could only manage a few unintelligible guttural sounds. Tremors wracked his body, even as perspiration beaded on his forehead. His eyes darted back and forth in their sockets, looking from Reid's face to the ground beside the chair—where nearly melted ice cubes and Billy's glass lay on the lawn, beside the radio that played a Reba McEntire song as if nothing was wrong.

And then Reid saw it—two bloody puncture wounds on the back of Billy's hand.

He met his friend's eyes. "Rattler."

Billy closed his eyes, and Reid took it to mean yes. "How long ago?"

If Billy knew, he couldn't say. Swelling and numbness had already set in, and so had the muscle spasms. Under normal circumstances, the snake bite would probably not be fatal. But these weren't normal circumstances. ALS had already weakened Billy's nervous and circulatory systems—the very things rattlesnake venom attacked.

Reid lifted Billy as gently as he could, and, hoisting him onto one shoulder, hotfooted it to the house. "Martina!" he bellowed. "Martina!"

As he entered the kitchen, he heard the vacuum cleaner roaring over the carpeting in the bedroom above.

No time to wait for her to finish the job, to run upstairs and pull the plug on the appliance. Under normal circumstances, he thought yet again, a person had four, maybe five hours to get help after a rattler bite. But as he'd already determined, these weren't normal circumstances; in Billy's already-weakened condition, only God knew how much time he had.

And Reid didn't intend to waste a single precious second.

He grabbed Martina's cell phone from the counter and headed straight back out the door to load Billy into the pickup. He wished he'd thought to grab the quilt Martina had draped over Billy out there in the yard, because if he remembered right, he was supposed to keep the man warm. Supposed to keep the bite site lower than the heart, too, he thought dialing 911. No way that was possible. Not unless he'd stuffed Billy into the bed of the pickup instead of the passenger seat.

He alerted the emergency room staff that a snakebite victim was on the way, added that the victim had

ALS, then dialed the ranch to tell Martina where he'd taken Billy. The phone rang and rang, and he cursed under his breath as the answering machine clicked on. Reid took a deep breath in a desperate attempt to keep the panic and fear out of his voice as he left his message. "Get one of the hands to drive you into town," he said before hanging up.

Because the poor woman sure wouldn't be in any shape to make the thirty-minute drive from the Rockin' C to Amarillo on her own.

Cammi had put off making the call long enough. She owed him an apology, owed him a sincere thank you, too. Dressed and showered, she felt a little more like her old self. It would take time, she knew, for the pain of losing the baby to diminish, but she had faith to get her through it now...thanks to Reid.

Was she giving him too much credit? Cammi wondered as she dialed the Rockin' C number. Would she have come to her senses on her own, in time?

Probably, she admitted as the number connected. But what if she'd made yet another mistake in the meantime, and it separated her even further from the Father?

"Martina? What's wrong?" she asked when her friend answered.

The woman sobbed hysterically. Near as Cammi could make out, someone had been bitten by a rattlesnake. Martina had mentioned Reid and Billy in quick succession. Her mouth went dry. "You need a ride to the hospital?"

Something about a ranch hand taking her burbled out, before Martina hung up.

Growing up on a Texas ranch means learning a thing or two about rattlers—where they like to hide, how they hunt prey, how to protect against a bite. Death was rare, very rare, Cammi knew. Reid was strong and healthy and would probably survive, even if treatment wasn't administered right after a snakebite. But Billy...

Cammi didn't want to think what might happen to a man already weakened by a terminal illness.

Lily slammed in through the back door and grabbed a cup of coffee. "What's up?"

"Can you drive me to the hospital?"

Lily's eyes widened. "Why? What's wrong with you?"

"Nothing's wrong with me. I'm fine." She grabbed a jacket from the small closet beside the back door. "It's Billy. Or Reid."

Lily grimaced. "Maybe you should've let us take you to the E.R. last night, because you're not making a lick of—"

"I just talked to Martina," Cammi interrupted, scribbling a note to her father. "She was too hysterical to make much sense, but near as I can tell, a rattler bit one of them."

Scooping her car keys from the counter, Lily opened the back door. "Let's make tracks, sis!"

They barely said a word during the drive from River Valley to Amarillo. "Hasn't been long since you were a patient here, yourself. Think the E.R. staff will recognize you?" Lily said, parking the car.

"I doubt it. But I'd wager they'd recognize Reid. He's a real rabble-rouser when things don't go his way."

"What do you mean?" Lily asked as they hurried toward the E.R. entrance.

Cammi explained how he'd barked orders like a drill sergeant the day she'd had her miscarriage.

They'd just crossed into the lobby when Lily said, "I like that guy. You let this one get away, you're crazy."

She might have agreed, if she hadn't seen Martina, huddled and trembling in a chair near the "Staff Only" doors. In seconds, the woman was flanked by London daughters.

"How is he?" Cammi started, hating herself even as she hoped it wasn't Reid who'd been bitten.

Slump-shouldered and red-eyed, Martina seemed cried out. Her voice was still sob-thick when she said, "Reid's in there with him. He wanted a minute alone with his boy."

Lily slid an arm around her shoulder. "Can I get you anything? Cup of coffee? Orange juice?"

Patting the younger woman's hand, Martina shook her head. "I'm just fine, dear, but thank you." She met Cammi's eyes, then grasped her hand. "Will you do something for me, Cammi?"

"'Course I will. Anything. Just name it." And she meant every word.

"Will you go back there, be with him…Reid, I mean?" She bit her lip as the tears welled up again, and daubed at her eyes with a wrinkled tissue. "I can't watch Billy—" she bit her lower lip before continuing "—and Reid shouldn't have to, at least, not all alone."

Cammi sat, slack-jawed and holding her breath. She was about to say, of course, she'd stay with Reid, for as long as he needed her, when Martina interrupted with "My Billy is dying. I've already said goodbye. The stubborn old fool doesn't want me to remember him this way." She smiled a little. "God love him." Sniffing, she added, "He wanted Reid, and nothing anyone said could change his mind."

Cammi's heart went out to Reid. Of course he'd grant Billy's last request, and be with him at the end. But it would be hard on him, so very hard....

"I can see by your face that you understand," Martina was saying. "I knew you were the right girl for Reid." A tear slid down her cheek and she brushed it away. "I've been praying for someone like you to come into his life, and I thank God for hearing my prayer!"

How like Martina to think of Reid at a time like this, instead of focusing on herself. Cammi could only hope she was made of that same sturdy, unselfish stuff, so that when loved ones needed *her*—

"Go to him, Cammi," Martina said. "He loves Billy like a father. They've been best friends for so long, it's hard to remember a time when they weren't part of one another's lives." She released Cammi's hand, waved her away. "He doesn't know it yet, but he needs you. Needs you more than he's ever needed anyone."

Cammi got to her feet and backed away. She met Lily's damp eyes. "Go on," her sister said. "I'll stay right here." She gave Martina a sideways hug. "Maybe we'll walk down to the chapel, sit in the quiet for a while." Another sideways hug, then, "And maybe we'll get some coffee in the cafeteria."

When Martina nodded, Cammi left them and

walked woodenly toward the "Staff Only" entrance. Her hands were trembling when the doors opened, her legs wobbly as she moved into the E.R. When she spotted Reid, Cammi took a deep breath and stood up straight, determined to look the part, at least, of someone who'd shown up to lend support. She stepped up behind him. For several moments, she stood stock-still, trying to decide how to let him know she was there. A touch? A word?

Without turning, he found her hand and gripped it tight, telling her he'd known all along that she was behind him. It moved her, and she expressed it by squeezing back.

"…not one for purty words," Billy struggled to say, "…but you're…like a son."

Reid swallowed. "Pretty syrupy stuff," he said, "for a guy who's not into sweet talk."

Billy's faint smile proved he got the joke. "Martina…she's gonna need you, son…."

He cleared his throat. "Don't worry, I won't let you down."

"I know…you never have. The ranch…you'll take care of—"

"You know I will, as if it's my own."

"Is."

"What?"

"Yours."

Cammi felt Reid's hand tense, felt the heat radiating from his palm to hers. He let go of her, but only long enough to slide an arm around her waist and pull her close to his side.

"What kind of drugs are they giving you?" he said on a dry, grating laugh. "You're spoutin' nonsense."

Billy gave one weak shake of his head and said, "No."

Reid shook his head, too. "But Billy, what about Martina? She's put as much of herself into that place as you ha—"

"Her idea." A shudder went through him before he continued. "Mexico…"

"She wants to go back to Mexico?"

One slight nod, then, "Mama, sisters…big ol' loving Hispanic family…"

Reid hung his head. "Billy," he said, grabbing the man's hand, "I—"

"Y'always did talk too much." Somehow, he found the strength to chuckle quietly, to open one eye and look at Reid. "Love you, son."

Reid pressed both hands on the mattress beside Billy's frail body, then balled them into fists. Cammi blanketed the nearest one with her hand, slipped an arm around his waist. Was her being here making this harder for him, she wondered, or easier? What would he be doing if she hadn't come?

"Love you, too, y'ornery ol' codger."

Billy laughed softly. "Told you—call me 'old' again, I'd take…take the strap to your—"

A moment passed while Billy closed his eyes—resting, it seemed. Reid smoothed a strand of hair over his friend's bald head. It was such a sweet, loving gesture that it brought tears to Cammi's eyes.

"That the li'l gal?" Billy rasped.

"This is Cammi," Reid said.

Billy lifted his head from the pillow and looked directly at her, both blue eyes blazing with determination. "Take care of him," he said. He lay back, spent by his short speech. One half of his mouth lifted in a mischievous grin. "Won't be easy, but…"

Another moment passed, with nothing but the *blip* and *bleep* of the monitors and Billy's labored breathing to disturb the absolute silence.

The older man lifted his head again, found Cammi's eyes. "Be good to him, girl." And then Billy slept.

Cammi stood silently by Reid's side, knowing that when words were necessary, God would tell her what he needed to hear. Meanwhile, she moved a little closer.

He pulled away from her long enough to press a kiss to Billy's forehead. "Rest well, y'old bear of a man," he said, voice thick with a pent-up sob.

Then he turned to Cammi and said, "Come to the chapel with me?"

Chapter Eleven

If Reid had ever doubted the power of prayer before, he didn't doubt it now! The congregation started a prayer chain for Billy's healing, and even the doctors couldn't explain his miraculous recovery.

Nearly a month after Billy got home from the hospital, Martina packed up, intent on moving them into her widowed sister's house, permanently.

Grateful as he was to have his old friend back, hale and hearty, Reid's heart ached. "I can't believe you're doing this," he said, staring at his hands.

Billy and Martina flanked him in black bucket seats at the airport's departure gate. "Billy and I discussed this long before he got sick," she explained. "We want you to have the Rockin' C, because we've always thought of you as our son. Besides, you worked it as if it was your own."

He wanted to ask how they'd get along, down in Acapulco, so far from church friends.

"We saved up for years, just for a day like this.

We're thinking of it as an adventure, so stop looking so sad! We're not rocketing to another planet, you know.'' She pinched his cheek. ''We'll come visit every chance we get, and so will you.''

The ticket agent's nasal monotone voice announced their flight.

She wrapped Reid in a long, motherly hug. ''I'll miss you, too.'' Standing, Billy grabbed their carry-on bag. ''Well, I guess this is it,'' he said. ''We'll call every week.''

Wagging a maternal finger under his nose, Martina added, ''The phone works both ways, don't forget!''

Reid nodded.

''Now go on home.'' Billy gave Reid's shoulder a fatherly squeeze.

He watched them move up in the line, and grinned when they turned to wave a final goodbye before disappearing into the tunnel that would lead them to the Mexico-bound 747.

Home she'd said. The Rockin' C wouldn't be the same without her and Billy and Martina, and neither would the big old house. Reid doubted he'd ever think of it as home, or the ranch as his.

He'd always been a loner, so it surprised Reid to learn he'd developed a dislike for being alone. That first week without Billy, without Martina, seemed longer than a lifetime.

Much as he'd wanted to, he hadn't called Cammi. When he saw her again, Reid wanted to be certain he was feeling more like himself.

It had been nearly three weeks since he'd set eyes on her. She had her car back, and his truck hadn't been damaged as badly as they'd both assumed. But she hadn't driven to the Rockin' C, and he hadn't made the trip to River Valley Ranch. It had been three of the longest weeks he'd ever spent. If anyone had told him it was possible to miss anyone this much, he would have said they'd gone haywire. Finally, he gave in to the never-ending yearning and dialed her number.

"So how's school?" he asked when she answered.

"It's just what the doctor ordered."

Hearing her voice was just what he needed. "Why's that?"

"Kids are so energetic, so enthusiastic, so full of life." She paused. "Puts things in perspective, you know?"

He took it to mean she missed the baby less, thanks to the distractions of being a busy teacher. Reid could almost picture her, smiling thoughtfully as she played with the phone cord. "So you like kids?"

"Like 'em?" Cammi laughed. "I absolutely *love* them."

With a personality like hers, she had to be great with kids. The elementary schoolers who called her Mrs. Carlisle probably gathered 'round her as if she were the Pied Piper. Then, from out of nowhere, the image of her sitting in a big wooden rocker with a baby at her breast flit through his mind. With a heart like hers, she'd be a terrific mother, he knew.

Suddenly, an overwhelming desire to tell her so filled him to overflowing. "I know it's last minute, but how 'bout letting me buy you dinner tonight?" He'd take her someplace where the lights were low and the waiters slung white towels over their tuxedo sleeves, where the music wafted quietly, and reflected candlelight would glitter in her big doe eyes.

She didn't answer soon enough to suit him. He hoped it was because she had papers to grade, a lesson plan to adjust. He didn't know if he could stand to hear anything else.

"I can't have dinner," she said at last, "but I'd like to see you."

There was a certain hesitancy, and the music he'd come to recognize as her voice, well, it wasn't quite as melodic as he remembered. Reid hoped it was temporary, that once she fully adjusted to being a widow, to losing her baby…

"I can pick you up in half an hour."

Another pause. If he didn't know better, Reid would've thought he'd dialed the wrong number.

"How about if I meet you in the park across from Georgia's Diner? I can be there in, oh, forty-five minutes."

The park? At this hour? "You're sure I can't treat you to dinner."

"No, really." She sighed. "I appreciate it, but I have thirty-odd book reports and math quizzes to grade before I turn in tonight."

He breathed a sigh of relief. "Still, it's kinda chilly to be meeting in the park, don't you think?"

A second ticked by, then two, before she said, "Maybe. But we won't be there for very long. See you in a little while, then."

Reid stared at the buzzing receiver for a full second after she hung up, wondering why he had the sneaking suspicion he was about to walk into a trap.

* * *

It was almost dark by the time she pulled into the parking space beside Reid's truck. Streetlights reflected eerily from slides and seesaws, and the wind shoved leather-seated swings, clanking their thick chains against hollow A-frame supports. She and Reid were the only two who'd braved the cold on this blustery November night.

He'd swapped his Stetson for a baseball cap, his denim jacket for one of thick down. When he walked toward her, she saw that he'd traded his pointy-toed cowboy boots for well-worn running shoes that left waffled footprints in the sand beneath the jungle gym.

"It's good to see you," he said when he reached her.

"Same here." And it was true. Which would only make what she had to say all the harder.

He stuffed his hands into his pockets and smiled nervously. If she didn't know better, Cammi would have said someone had tipped him off, because it seemed he sensed why she'd asked him to meet her here.

"How're you holding up?"

Reid stared at the toes of his sneakers, nodding. "Fine, fine." He looked up. "House seems strange without them. I didn't realize how quiet the place could be until…" He went back to staring at his feet. "How 'bout you?" he said. "Is everything okay?"

He referred to the miscarriage, of course. "Fine, fine," she echoed. How sad that it had come to this awkward perfunctory conversation, like they were strangers who'd ended up in the same line at the grocery store. Especially sad when she considered how warm things had been between them before Billy's ordeal.

She saw him lift his shoulders and pull his coat collar up around his ears. "Let's sit in my car," she suggested. "At least we'll be out of the wind."

His eyes locked on hers. "I—"

Reid clamped his lips together, a hint that he'd decided against saying whatever had been on his mind. Cammi got into her car and sat behind the wheel. Almost immediately, Reid slid into the passenger seat.

"All right, so let's have it," he said, his voice flat and emotionless.

"Have what?"

He turned slightly to face her, one brow up, one side of his mouth down. "I think it's safe to say you didn't ask me here on a night like this to invite me to the prom."

Blinking, Cammi bit her lower lip. "You're right. I asked you here to say…" But she couldn't say. Not just yet, anyway.

"…that you missed me?" he finished on a bitter chuckle.

Cammi sighed. "Reid."

He looked at the car's ceiling. "I've thought about you almost nonstop since Billy and Martina left." Eyes on her again, he said, "I know it sounds crazy, considering we've only known one another a few weeks, but I want—"

It wouldn't be fair to let him say it, considering what she'd have to say next. To protect his feelings, his ego, she held up a hand to stop him. "I've been doing a lot of thinking. I agree with you, about how fast things have progressed between us—I mean, because I feel the same way.''

The sadness lifted like a curtain of smoke, and his face brightened, his eyes glittered. Smiling, Reid said, ''I was hoping you'd say that.'' He took her hand in his. ''Whew,'' he said on a laugh. ''You really had me going there for a minute!''

He'd misunderstood her, completely. The point she'd been trying to make was that *despite* how she felt about him after such a short time—or maybe *because* it had been such a short time—she'd done some serious thinking. And it wasn't just that. It was the dreams and images, the pictures that flashed in her mind every time she saw him.

She hadn't made her decision in haste, the way she'd made so many others. Because this time, she needed to be right, for Reid's sake more than her own.

''You deserve so much better than the likes of me, Reid. You ought to have a woman in your life who will love and cherish—''

''Look me in the eye and tell me you don't love me.''

His voice was hard, his eyes mere slits. He was hurting, and it showed, in the taut line of his mouth, in the furrows on his brow. She couldn't tell him she didn't love him, though she'd rehearsed it a hundred times. Couldn't say the words because…because she *did* love him, more than life itself!

Unfortunately, that didn't change the ugly facts.

''This is the hardest thing I've ever had to do in my life,'' she admitted, slowly, deliberately, ''because in all honesty…'' Yes, she loved him. Loved him with all her heart. Because he was the kind of man she'd been dreaming about since junior high school, the kind who was strong and capable, yet tender at the same time. If only *that* image overshadowed the others....

"You deserve better than a woman who sees what I see when I'm with you." She shook her head. "It just wouldn't be fair."

He sat quietly for some moments, shaking his head, shrugging, as if replaying the whole scene over and over in his head. "So what you're saying, then, is that when you look at me, you see your poor mama, the way she was that night. And since it's my fault she's dead, you're telling me we're over before we began...but it's all for *my* sake."

There was no mistaking the sarcasm in his voice, and frankly, Cammi couldn't blame him. Because it did sound ridiculous when he put it that way. Unfortunately, that didn't change things. He'd carried the burden of guilt for her mother's death all these many years. She wouldn't add to it now by letting him think such a thing.

She laid a hand on his forearm, felt him stiffen when she touched him, as if trying to prevent himself from recoiling. But she ignored it, gave his forearm a gentle squeeze. "It isn't you, Reid, it's me. Call me a fickle female, an overly sensitive idiot, a weak-kneed little brat. But I need time, that's all—time to sort things out." She shrugged. "So much has happened, to both of us, in these past few weeks. If only you'd give me some time."

He faced forward, staring through the windshield, nodding. "Time," he told the darkness enshrouding them. "She needs time."

Cammi could fix it all, could straighten out this misunderstanding by telling the truth, by saying three little words. But *if* she said them, he'd never let her go, because he believed he loved her. But did he? Or had he confused being her hero for the real thing?

Reid was a good man, a decent man, and he deserved the chance to find out for sure. Deserved a chance to share his life with a woman who'd saved herself just for him, who'd never been married or carried another man's child, who wasn't forever letting her "act first, think later" mind-set get her into trouble!

"Guess I'd better go, then," he said. He started to get out of the car, then got back in and closed the door again. "Will you do me one favor before I leave?"

"Sure," she said. "Anything."

Smiling a sad little smile, he said, "One more for the road?"

It's what he'd said that night in her kitchen, before taking her in his arms. Cammi's heart fluttered, just remembering it.

Reid leaned forward, tenderly held her face in his hands, studying her eyes, her cheeks, her forehead. He stroked her hair, then buried his face in it, as if trying to imprint every detail in his memory. Then he shifted and, closing his own eyes, he kissed her. Soft. Sweet. Filled with so much tenderness and meaning that she almost forgot the message she'd come here to deliver.

"Take care, Cammi."

Before she could object, or change her mind, or

agree, he was gone, and she knew the chilly wind wasn't the only reason she shivered.

Cammi leaned her forehead on the steering wheel, and prayed she hadn't just made the biggest mistake of her life.

Reid paced the darkened ranch house till long past midnight, reliving those moments in the front seat of Cammi's car. When he had taken her face in his hands and looked into her eyes, and challenged her to say she didn't love him, he had expected her to bend like a cheap spoon. *Good thing you're not a betting man,* he thought, frowning.

He'd stayed away these past weeks more for her sake than his own. Saying goodbye to Martina and Billy had taken a lot out of him, but his distress paled by comparison to what Cammi had gone through these past few months.

She sure had him convinced she loved him, looking at him with those soulful eyes, sighing each time their lips met—and standing beside him at the hospital when Billy struggled to live. Then, with no warning or explanation, she'd backed away, emotionally and physically.

She'd been straightforward about her reasons, he had to give her that. She'd been hurt and humiliated by Rusty—added to the pain of losing a baby, well, was it any wonder she wanted to be careful this time, to protect herself from repeating the same mistakes?

She needed time, he'd decided, to salt things out, to figure out this…what was happening between them. Knowing she was too big-hearted to ask for it, Reid gave her time, and plenty of space, too. Which hadn't been easy, what with the phone always in easy reach and River Valley on the way to or from just about every place he'd driven these long, tormenting weeks.

It had been missing her that weakened him enough to cut his "keep your distance for a couple of months" plan by weeks. When he called to ask her to dinner, Cammi had sounded…peculiar, not at all her usual spunky, live-wire self. Maybe she was miffed, he'd told himself, *because* he'd waited so long to call. All he needed was a few minutes, face-to-face, to explain that he'd stayed away for her own good….

Looking back on it, Reid had to admit that it seemed more than a little strange when she asked him to meet her at the park. But what he knew about women you could put in one eye; maybe she thought meeting there would be romantic! Then, when he first saw Cammi, slender shoulders hunched into the wind and dark hair fluttering, his heart thumped so hard he wondered if a man had ever died of longing, 'cause he sure had wanted to make her his own, right then and there!

Had Cammi truly been cold, he wondered now, when she suggested they sit in her car? Or was she simply guaranteeing a quick getaway once she'd delivered her speech?

Reid stopped pacing, stood in the middle of the living room between Martina's easy chair and Billy's favorite recliner. He could almost picture them—Martina knitting, Billy working on a fishing lure—chatting amiably about the TV news, ranch business, the weather. They'd always sounded more like lifelong pals to him than a couple who'd been married more than half their lives.

The Stones had taught him a lot, right here in this room, important life lessons about always giving his all-out best to any job he might tackle, about doing the right thing, even when it hurt. He'd learned something else from them, too—something they might not have realized they'd taught him.

Not *all* marriages are rife with anger and accusation, like his mother's had been; some—like Martina and Billy's—were rooted in trust and respect, brimming with warmth and affection. Adversity and strife only strengthened the bonds of their love, and made Reid believe that someday, with the right woman, he, too could have a marriage like that.

The right woman, he believed, was Cammi. Or could have been.

Driving his fingers through his hair, Reid groaned, feeling caught between the proverbial rock and a hard place. He wanted a life with Cammi more than he'd ever wanted anything. But he'd never have it. Why? Because one look at him and she would always be reminded of that terrible night....

He slammed a fist into his palm, knowing even as he did so that the fit of temper was pointless. He had no one but himself to blame for the sorry state of his life. If he hadn't always avoided commitment—and who was he kidding?—hadn't always avoided *love*, he might already have a wife and kids. If he'd had a family of his own on the night Cammi Carlisle crashed into his life...

That idea only frustrated him more, since Cammi was the only woman he'd ever considered sharing his

life with. Her carefully rehearsed speech had cut deep,
hurt worse than anything old Ruthless had done that
day in the bullring. He'd spend the rest of his days
as a hermit before he'd put himself in the line of fire
that way again.

Still…living out the rest of his life alone…

Confused, frustrated, angry, heartbroken… Until
Cammi, Reid hadn't known a man could experience
so many emotions, all at the same time!

He stepped onto the porch, hoping a few minutes
in the crisp cool air would clear his head, help him
come up with a solution for his problem.

And the dilemma, as he saw it, was whether to stay
at the Rockin' C, or leave Amarillo, this time for
good. It would be the toughest decision he'd ever
make, because the ranch had been the only real home
he'd ever known, Billy and Martina the only real family. This was his land now, to do with as he saw fit.
Selling it was not an option, not after all the sweat
and tears Billy had put into it.

The distant notes of a coyote's cry pierced the om-
inous black silence. Instinctively, Reid narrowed his
eyes. Every nerve end prickled, every muscle tensed
as he scanned the horizon. The critter was out there
somewhere, probably perched high atop a mesa and
silhouetted by the crescent moon. He had good reason
to fear the mangy thief, for coyotes were cunning—
costly, too, in the damage they caused to livestock.

But this night, the mournful wail touched something in Reid, a long-forgotten primal chord that rang
with the most basic of truths. Over the centuries, man
and beast had come to see one another as the enemy.
Yet despite eons-long battles over territory, the two

had one thing, at least, in common. The stealthy hunter's cries were rooted in the most primitive of needs; he yearned for a life mate, for the comfort that is best satisfied by the bonds of companionship. Understanding that, Reid said a quick hopeful prayer that the sad-songed animal would find what it was searching for. "One of us oughta get some happiness in this lifetime," he said into the wind.

He headed back inside with more questions than answers. Should he re-up with the rodeo? If his shoulder gave out during a hard ride, he'd lose his balance and end up eating dust, end up permanently crippled…or worse.

Or should he stay?

A picture flashed in his mind: Cammi, on the arm of another man..one who wouldn't be a constant reminder of a sad and painful part of her past..smiling and happy with her new life. Nothing a saddle bronc or a bull could do to him would hurt anywhere near as much as that. And sooner or later, that life was bound to happen to her, because if ever a woman was born to be a wife and mother, it was Cammi!

So it was decided, then: Come first light, he'd have a long talk with Hank, best ranch hand Reid ever had the pleasure of working with, bar none. He'd promise a bigger paycheck and permission to move into the house in exchange for acting as overseer of the Rockin' C. That way, years from now, when time and distance dulled the pain of losing her, Reid would have a place to call home.

Meanwhile, he'd pull the old cab out of the shed and reattach it to the bed of his pickup. Sure, he had

enough money for hotel rooms, but what more did he
need than a bedroll for himself and oats for his horse?
Till the day came when he could think of Cammi and
not want to weep like a child, it would do just fine.

Chapter Twelve

Cammi couldn't believe her ears. "What do you mean, he's gone?"

"I mean, he left here more'n six months ago," said the man who'd answered Reid's phone.

She'd asked him for time that night in the park, and as the calendar pages turned, Cammi thanked him in her prayers for giving it to her. She'd made this phone call, hoping against hope that he still felt the way he had the last time she saw him.

"But I—I don't understand."

"Sorry, lady. Don't know what else t'tell you."

Surely Reid wouldn't have walked away from the Rockin' C. Not after what Billy had put into it. "Who's running the ranch?"

"That'd be me. Name's Jefford, Hank Jefford."

Cammi couldn't bear to ask the question, for fear of the answer. "Reid…sold you the Rockin' C?"

A dry chuckle filtered into her ear. "No, ma'am. Hired me. I'm the overseer."

It simply didn't make sense. No sense at all. "Did he say where he was going?"

"Signed himself up with the rodeo."

The breath caught in her throat. Hadn't Martina said Reid's shoulder injury was severe? Damaged enough that another fall could cause permanent damage…or a fatality? "Why would he do such a thing?"

"Never asked, and he never said."

Stunned, Cammi couldn't speak.

"Looked to me like ol' Reid got his heart broke."

She swallowed. "What makes you say that?"

"Not just me that says it. Fellers 'round here claim to have seen him with a purty li'l dark-haired gal, and since she ain't been 'round of late, my guess is she's the reason he hightailed it out of town."

Cammi's heart knocked against her ribs. Had Reid left because she…because she'd broken his heart? But how could that be, she thought, frowning, when they'd only spent a short time together?

Then she remembered the way he'd taken care of her after the miscarriage. Remembered that night in her kitchen, and after the fall near the barn, and those electric-quiet moments in her car when she'd asked him for time….

"Do you have any idea how I might get in touch with him?"

"Well," Hank drawled, "he moves around a good bit."

Exasperated, Cammi blurted, "Surely he left a number, or calls from time to time to see how things are going." *Please, God,* she prayed, *let this man know where I can find Reid!*

"He was in Durango last time he checked in. Said somethin' 'bout movin' on to Butte."

Montana? "When?" For all she knew, Reid had already been killed in a fall, or stomped to death by a Brahman.

"Oh, 'bout a month or so ago, I reckon."

She thanked Hank and hung up, then hid behind her hands. What kind of hideous, horrible woman causes that kind of damage to a man's ego—and doesn't even know it! Cammi's cheeks burned with shame, her heart pounded with guilt. If she'd told Reid the truth that night when he'd taken her face in his hands…if she'd admitted right then how much she loved him…

These past months had changed things, and prayer had answered her questions. She loved Reid, there was no getting around that. She'd wasted so much precious time, sticking her head in the sand to hide from her fears, to hide from the self-imposed guilt at how being with Reid might hurt her family. Now, it was time to face life, head-on.

She'd called the Rockin' C to explain all this to Reid, to cite her ludicrous reasons for avoiding him, to beg his forgiveness, to tell him how long and hard she'd prayed that he'd at least think about picking up where they left off.

She hadn't expected to find out he'd given up everything rather than face life without her. The notion humbled Cammi, because she didn't deserve to be loved that strongly, that deeply, especially not after the immature, self-centered way she'd behaved!

She had to find him—the sooner the better!—and try to make him understand.

But *if* she managed to find him, would he still feel the same way? Or had loneliness made him replace her with one of the willing females who followed the rodeo, hoping to win a trophy of their own?

There was only one way to find out.

Spring break would begin on Monday, so there'd be no need to ask for time off from school.

Retracing Reid's steps would be easy compared to explaining her plans to her father. Somehow, she had to make Lamont understand that she owed it to Reid to make things right. There was a chance the cowboy would send her packing—but maybe a miracle would happen.

Cammi headed upstairs to throw some things into a suitcase. She packed enough to last a good long while, because she didn't intend to come back until she'd found Reid and made her peace with him.

God willing, he'd still be healthy enough to hear it.

Bareback riding, Reid thought, standing near the bucking chute, was like trying to ride a twelve-hundred-pound jackhammer, holding on with only one hand.

Sheer strength alone wouldn't keep him on the horse. He had to spur just enough, turn his toes outward at exactly the right degree, make an educated guess how far down the animal's shoulders his feet should hang—until those pounding front hooves hit the ground after exploding from the chute. After that, he could only grab tight to the rigging, lean back and take whatever punishment the brute decided to dish out.

Spectators had jam-packed the arena, whooping and hollering as the announcer's booming baritone echoed through the stands: *"Ladies and gentlemen, I'd like to draw your attention to Chute Number Two, where Gold Buckle award-winner Reid Alexander is going for another All-Around win on the back of Malicious, one of the meanest, orneriest, buckin'-est equines on four legs...."*

The crowd stood, applauding and whistling in support of their favorite rodeo cowboy. "Get 'im, Reid!" shouted one fan. "Show 'im who's boss!" bellowed another. Their cheers woke the showman in Reid, and he gave them what they wanted—waving his hat in the air with one hand, throwing a punch with the other.

"The last rodeo cowboy who rode Malicious," the announcer continued, *"got himself freight-trained. Let's hope this animal won't run over Reid that a-way in this go-round!"*

Privately, Reid hoped the same thing. He'd seen this horse at work—definitely not a scooter, content to pivot without bucking. No such luck! Malicious liked to suck back, changing direction in a split second. He liked to crow-hop, too—jumping stiff-legged that way guaranteed the fans would see daylight between Reid's rear end and the horse's back. If that wasn't bad enough, Malicious was a star gazer, too. Every cowboy knew it spelled disaster, because it was near impossible to keep the slack out of the reins when a horse bucked with its head up that way. Yep, Malicious was a good bucker, all right. If Reid could hold his own here, maybe he really *could* pick up where he'd left off.

He didn't want to admit, not even to himself, that he was bone-tired, that his shoulder ached almost as much as it had when he'd first left the hospital. But what did he expect, after testing its limits by entering the Keyhole Race, the Straight-Away Barrels, and the Mad Mouse…for starters. Entering the Bareback event in this condition was as good as asking for a stint in the local hospital.

"Better hike up them shotguns," another cowboy advised.

Nodding, Reid adjusted the belt of his step-in chaps, then tugged at the hems of his leather gloves.

"You reckon ever'thing we hear 'bout this brute is a windy?" the cowboy asked.

No, the tales spun about *this* horse were factual. He'd seen the proof of it with his own eyes. Reid pressed the Stetson tighter onto his head. "I ain't that lucky," he said, only half joking.

Chuckling, the cowboy cuffed him on the back. "Ready?"

Reid nodded again, grabbed the wall and threw one leg over. "Ready as I'll ever—"

"Reid!"

He stopped so fast, the spur on his boot sang a whining, one-note tune as it spun round and round. Cammi? But how could that be, way out here, after all these months? *You're losin' it, old man*—he thought as he continued to lever himself above the chute.

"How'd that li'l gal get in here?" the annoyed cowboy asked, as Reid hovered above the snorting, frenzied animal. "Lady, you ain't allowed down—"

"Reid, don't do it!"

It was Cammi, all right. But how she got here—
and why—were questions he couldn't afford to ask
himself right now. He had to concentrate on the
ride…concentrate on the ride…on the ride….

She shoved past the cowboy and peered over the
wall. "Why are you doing this, Reid?" she demanded. "Your shoulder! The rodeo can't be paying
you enough to risk—"

He didn't hear the rest, because down there in the
chute it was more obvious than ever how Malicious
had come by his name. The horse wheezed and
huffed, hard muscles rippling in a desperate bid to get
out into the open, to get Reid off his back.

Cammi's voice echoed in his mind. She sounded
scared, real scared, but that didn't surprise him; a
born-and-bred rancher's daughter had seen enough ro-
deos to know what he was risking, tackling a horse
like this in his condition. Reid wanted to tell her to
go home, to quit worrying about his shoulder. But the
clock was ticking now. Too late to change his mind,
even if he wanted to. And he didn't want to. Because
he hadn't come back to the rodeo just for the day
money.

She'd been so glad to see him that it was all Cammi
could do to contain herself. She wanted to scream his
name, burst through the crowd of cowboys standing
around him, wrap her arms around him and give him
a kiss he'd never forget.

He looked so handsome standing there, dusty boot
tips poking out from the hem of his flare-bottomed
brown chaps. He'd fastened all but the top snap of
his green plaid western shirt, and the tails of the white

bandanna wrapped around his throat rested on one shoulder. His biceps bulged as he tugged at worn leather gloves, flexed again as he adjusted the black Stetson so that it shaded his deeply tanned face.

Thank you, God! she prayed, grateful she'd found him, thankful to see him looking hearty and all in one piece. "Reid!"

It seemed he hadn't heard her, so she moved closer, called to him again. This time, he locked onto her eyes with that so-green gaze of his. She smiled, waved again, expecting him to look at least slightly happy to see her.

Instead, Reid's brows drew together in the center of his forehead, one side of his mouth turning down before he returned his attention to the bucking beast in the chute.

Bareback riding was one of the most dangerous events of the rodeo, even for cowboys without injuries. For Reid...

She couldn't let him do it. Couldn't understand why he'd *want* to! Cammi shoved past the cowboys assigned to keep the horse under control until the gate opened, and called to him again, demanded to know what he thought he was doing down there.

If he heard her, he gave no sign. Reid clenched his jaw and lowered himself onto the horse's back, got himself into position.

"Ready?" one cowboy asked. Reid gave a quick nod, and with his knees pressing into the animal's flanks and nothing to hold on to but the suitcase handle near the animal's neck, he threw his free hand in the air, gloved forefinger pointing toward the heavens—and gave the signal.

The wooden doors flew open...

...and Malicious charged forward, bound and determined to get rid of his rider. He was a beautiful animal, charcoal gray with a long black tail and a sleek black mane. He was grace and power personified, with glistening muscles that strained with every kick, twisting and turning with eyeblink speed.

The next seconds ticked by in a blur, a flurry of rib-racking noise and heart-pounding danger. She squinted through the fog of dust churned up by the horse's hooves, praying Reid would make it safely through this event.

"Uh-oh," the announcer yelled through the P.A. system, *"looks like Malicious is provin' how he got his name, again. Our boy Reid is down."*

Cammi scrambled past the cowboys and rodeo clowns, past the on-call doctor, and knelt in the dirt beside him. "Reid," she said, cradling his head in her lap. Blood oozed from a deep gash in his forehead, and his left leg lay twisted at an odd angle.

He looked into her face and smiled slightly, opened his bloodied lips and tried to say something before pain made him squeeze his eyes shut.

"Shh," Cammi said, smoothing the hair back from his brow. "Just rest easy, 'cause the ambulance is on its way."

"Doesn't look good," she heard the doctor tell one of the barrel men. "Better have the announcer get something else going until we can get him off the field."

Please, God... she prayed, blinking back stinging tears. *Watch over him. Keep him safe. Let him be all right!*

* * *

The E.R. docs had rushed Reid straight to surgery, where he spent the next six hours. Two hours later, they wheeled him from recovery and assigned him a room on the fifth floor. Cammi spent the night curled up in the high-backed vinyl chair beside his hospital bed, waking every time he so much as flinched.

Warm sunshine, slanting through the narrow opening in the curtains, crossed the room like a buttery yardstick, measuring the distance from the window to where she dozed. Opening one eye, she yawned and stretched.

"How long have you been there?"

The suddenness of Reid's craggy voice startled her. Both palms pressed to her chest, she smiled. "You're awake!" Inching closer, she leaned on the mattress and gently took his bandaged hand in hers. "How're you feeling? Thirsty?" Grabbing the drinking glass from the nightstand, she held the bendable straw to his lips.

His eyes never left hers as he sipped. When he'd had his fill, Reid turned away. "How long have you been here?" he asked without looking at her.

"Oh," she said, smoothing his covers, "awhile."

"All night?"

She shrugged. "So what if I was?"

A raspy sigh hissed from him. "Go home, Cammi."

He sounded tired, sad, defeated all at the same time. Just the aftereffects of hours in the operating room, she thought. Just the pain medications. "I'm not going home or anywhere else until I know you're all right." And she meant it, too.

"Suit yourself," he said, still looking at the window.

"You never answered my question."

He closed his eyes and said a sleepy "What question?"

"How're you feeling? Does anything hurt? I can call your doctor."

Another sigh. "Still have one good hand," he told her, moving the fingers of his left hand. "If I need anything, I'll buzz a nurse."

He had a right to be angry with her. If it hadn't been for her self-centered remarks that night in the car, if she hadn't distracted him before he went into the arena this afternoon... It was Cammi's turn to sigh, because what had happened to him had been her fault.

The doctor said the fall had caused a concussion, a fractured shoulder blade, a broken thigh and shattered ankle, and a bad wrist sprain. And Malicious's hooves cracked three ribs—one of which had punctured a lung. "We'll keep him here for two or three days," the surgeon had said. "After that, he'll need bed rest for a couple of weeks."

And after that, Cammi knew, a wheelchair, followed by crutches, then a cane.

And she intended to nurse him right up until he felt like his old self again.

"Can't let you do that," Reid said when she announced her decision.

Using his good hand, he shoved himself upright in the bed. "Let me rephrase it, then." One brow high on his forehead, he said, "I don't *want* you to do that.'' He made a thin, taut line of his lips, as if to show her he meant business.

"Might as well get used to the idea." She plopped a stack of clean, fresh clothes on the foot of the bed.

"I won't get used to it!" He'd made the mistake of drumming his point home by punching his injured hand into the mattress. Wincing, he clenched his teeth. "Only way I'd move into Lamont London's house is in a pine box," he said once the pain dulled a bit. "I mean it, Cammi. I'm going home. To the Rockin' C. Got it?"

She folded both arms over her chest. "All right, then, I'll move a few of my things into *your* house, take care of you there until—"

"No."

He had every right to be angry with her, but had no right to abuse himself. "Hate me if you must," she said, narrowing her eyes, "but if Mohammad won't come to 'the London,' 'the London' will come to him!"

"Very funny."

He wasn't smiling, she noted. "Only way you can keep me outta there is by calling the sheriff." Grinning smugly, she shrugged. "Besides, it's all arranged. I've hired a man to drive your pickup back to the Rockin' C. He'll tow my car behind it. I tried to get a hold of Martina and Billy, but—"

"Leave them out of this. They've been through enough."

He'd been angry the night she ran the red light, and when Amanda foisted herself on him across from Georgia's Diner, and in her car, after she'd asked for time. But that had been a different kind of anger than what she was seeing now—a blend of resentment and frustration that turned his otherwise DJ-like voice cold, that changed his expression from welcoming to distant.

''I don't need your help,'' he tacked on, as if what he'd already said hadn't made his feelings clear enough.

His remark stung like a cold slap, but she hid it well, pretending to fuss with the clothes she'd laundered for him while waiting for his operation to end. How else *could* he react, when she knew as well as he did that it was her fault Reid lay flat on his back, broken and bruised in body and spirit!

It came to Cammi in a blinding, painful flash…

Every time Reid saw her face from this day forward, he'd be reminded of what his surgeon had said earlier: ''I'm afraid your rodeo days are over, this time for good, son. One more fall like that and you'll spend the rest of your days in a wheelchair—if you have any days to spend.''

The bitter irony throbbed and ached inside her, raising a sob in her throat, bringing tears to her eyes.

Cammi hoped and prayed she'd be able to make it up to him—and prayed Reid would give her the time to do it.

Chapter Thirteen

Reid was beginning to feel guilty about his grumpy attitude. True, he hurt in places he didn't even know he had, but that was no reason to take it out on Cammi. She'd worked tirelessly and cheerfully these past few weeks and he hadn't exactly been appreciative.

Just as she'd vowed on the day his surgeon signed the release forms, Cammi hadn't budged from his side. She had hired an ambulance to drive him from New Mexico to Amarillo, and when the driver had explained civilians weren't allowed in the back with patients, she had huffed and climbed inside anyway. "What're you gonna do," she spat when he repeated the rules, "call the cops?" Reid had sympathized with the driver, who gave up without a fight, shrugging as he closed the doors.

Every time they had hit a bump in the road, she'd patted his hand. "I'll bet that hurt!" she'd said, or "They need to do something about these roads!"

From the moment she set foot into the house, she'd taken charge, instructing Hank and the hands to re-arrange the living room furniture so the hospital bed she'd rented would fit. "Put it beside the windows," she told the hands, "so he can watch what's going on outside." She made it up with velvet-soft flannel sheets "so bed sores won't develop," and smoothed out every wrinkle with her tiny, hardworking hands.

She stood there, wincing as the men moved Reid from the ambulance gurney to the bed. "Careful," she kept saying. "Be gentle with him!" And when she dismissed them, Cammi shoved the big old console TV across the room—grunting quietly, her face a knot of stubborn determination as she struggled with it—so he wouldn't even have to turn his head to see the screen.

Each morning, when he opened his eyes, the first thing he saw was Cammi, dozing in the big easy chair beside his bed. And she was there, pretending to be engrossed in a novel, when he settled in for the night.

She'd left him from time to time, but only long enough to cook a meal or get a fresh glass of water to wash down his pain medication. She was in the kitchen now, fixing his supper. The delicious scents of something Italian wafted through the house, and Reid's stomach grumbled with anticipation.

The front door opened, then closed with a *bang*. "Evenin'," Lamont said. He took off his hat, laid it atop the floor lamp's shade. "Feelin' better?"

Reid nodded. "She lets me up a couple of times a day now, puts me in that contraption for an hour or two at a spell." He pointed at the wheelchair that stood near the entry.

"I should've warned you it wouldn't be a picnic. Not with my Cammi in charge."

Another nod. Reid's feelings toward the older man had changed, from grudging acceptance to quiet admiration. Though he had said it in plain English, Lamont was now trying to show Reid how sorry he was for the way he'd behaved in the E.R. all those years ago. For his own part, Reid had said in a roundabout way, months earlier when they'd met at the diner, that all was forgiven.

"Hi, Dad," Cammi sang as she entered the room. "I didn't hear you come in."

"Just got here," he admitted, grinning. "Whatever you're cookin' invited me all the way from River Valley." He nodded at Reid. "What's the boy's incentive to get back on his feet when you're treatin' him like a king every minute of the day!"

Cammi blushed so deeply that Reid could see it from across the room, despite the low lighting. "Just doing my job," she said, tidying Lamont's collar. "Will you join us for supper?"

Chuckling, her father said, "You'd have to hogtie me to keep me away from the table."

"Everything is ready. I'll set a place for you as soon as I help Reid into his…into the…" Shaking her head, she sighed.

Reid hated how uncomfortable she seemed, just saying the word *wheelchair*. He'd pretty much stopped taking the big white pain capsules prescribed by his surgeon, and as the drug-induced fog lifted, he saw a lot of things more clearly.

Those first days home from the hospital, he'd secretly blamed Cammi for the accident—and that was wrong, just plain wrong. Because down deep, he knew full well that what happened had been his own fault. He never should have entered the Bareback event in the first place, let alone after a long, hard day of competing in every contest offered. And the way she'd been behaving—fussing over him, doting on him, even when he barked at her, even when he behaved like a low-down ingrate—proved that she held herself far more accountable for his condition than he could in a month of Sundays.

It was high time the two of them laid their cards on the table. He'd decided, just this afternoon, to put it to her plain at supper tonight: He had nobody to blame but himself for the shape he was in. But since Lamont had agreed to share the meal, his announcement would have to wait.

Cammi rolled the wheelchair alongside the bed, exactly as she'd been doing for more than a week now. "I read up on this online," she'd announced that first day. "There's a system to getting this done with the least amount of strain on the patient." Then she proceeded to teach him "the system," step by step. First, Cammi cranked the bed's backrest to its full upright position and instructed him to sit up as straight as he could. Next, she helped him swing his legs over the edge of the mattress, and sat beside him, waiting till he draped an arm over her shoulders. Last, she stood slowly and easily, until his feet hit the floor. Cammi let him set the pace, acting as his support and his guide, until he could lower himself into the wheelchair's seat.

"Looks like the pair of you have that down to a fine science," Lamont said, grinning.

Reid chuckled. "Took some getting used to."

"Isn't that the truth!" Cammi draped a blanket over his lap. "He hates being waited on. Hates feeling helpless even more."

He'd never said that. Had tried not to complain about anything, as a matter of fact. So how had she known?

Dinner conversation was quietly pleasant, and Cammi sent Lamont home with the leftover half of a home-baked apple pie. He kissed her cheek, then shook Reid's good hand.

"When you get outta that contraption," he said, grinning, "you and I are gonna have a talk about your intentions toward my daughter—"

Cammi blushed again, even deeper than before. "Drive safely, Dad," she interrupted. Taking his hand, she led him to the door. "Sorry you had to eat and run, but…"

"…but here's your hat, what's your hurry," Lamont finished, laughing.

She stood there several seconds after closing the door, simply staring at the floor, as if trying to summon the courage to face Reid after what Lamont had said. Finally, she said, "I'm so sorry about that." She turned toward him. "I don't know what gets into him sometimes."

Reid only smiled.

"Want some help getting back into bed?"

He shook his head. "No." Pointing at the easy chair, he said, "Set a spell with me."

"I should really get busy on those dishes. That mozzarella cheese is like concrete once it hardens."

''The dishes are fine, soaking in the sink.'' He pointed at the chair again.

Cammi eased onto the seat and folded her hands on the knees of her jeans. ''So,'' she began, ''you okay? Need anything for pain?''

Chuckling, he took her hand. ''I'm fine. Well, I will be once I get this off my chest.''

She bit her lip, blinking and staring at him as if she expected him to light into her. Had he been *that* difficult to take care of?

''I owe you an apology,'' he said, reminding himself of the night they'd met, when he'd found himself saying he was sorry for bellowing. The accident had reminded him so much of the night that had changed the course of his life.

''An apology!'' Cammi giggled nervously. ''If anyone owes anyone an apology, it's—''

''Cammi, hush.''

''But you don't have a thing to—''

''Humor me, will ya?'' He'd said that before, too, the night that he'd carried her from the barn path to the house.

Her shoulders sagged slightly, and the expression on her pretty face said, ''Okay, shoot.''

''You've been great, Cammi. Everything you've done these past weeks…I wouldn't have gotten care like this from a full-time nurse. And don't think I don't know it!''

''It's the least I could do'' was her quiet response, ''since it's my—''

''Cammi, hush, remember?''

She clamped her lips together and raised her eyebrows. He could've kissed her for sitting there, looking for all the world like a penitent teenage girl. Maybe later, he thought; right now what he had to say was far more important.

He told her the fall from Malicious had been his own stupid fault, that he'd pushed himself too hard for too long, that his tired old body had simply seen hitting the dirt that day as the last and final straw. He admitted that, because he'd been mad at himself for making so many foolish choices—including the one that put him back on the rodeo circuit—he'd taken things out on her. "I should've done this a long time ago," he concluded, "because it isn't fair, letting you believe you're responsible."

"You wouldn't have left the Rockin' C in the first place if I hadn't said what I did to you."

"Hush," he said yet again. "You can't take the blame for that, either, pretty lady. I've had a lot of time to think on things, holed up in here the way I've been since my fall. Truth is, I'd been chompin' at the bit, lookin' for any excuse to get back to rodeoing. Something in me said if I'd just give it one more try, I'd find out the shoulder was strong enough, after all, that I could win a few more gold buckles before I hung up my spurs." He rolled the wheelchair closer to where she sat and gently chucked her chin. "Your li'l 'time' speech gave me just the excuse I needed."

Her dark eyes filled with tears and her lower lip began to quiver.

"Aww, Cammi," he said, palm to her cheek. "What is it? Why're you cryin'?"

She pressed into his touch, like a feral cat that, starved for affection, leans into the first person to show it some kindness.

"You're such a big-hearted guy," she said, sniffing. "What a nice thing to do—taking the blame on your own shoulders to spare me carrying the burden." She turned her face slightly, kissed his palm. "I love you for that."

Had he heard right? Heart pounding, Reid smiled. He hadn't felt as pleased or relieved in… He couldn't remember feeling happier! It started a chain reaction of words, and unable to stop himself, he said, "This is gonna sound like a line from a B-grade movie, but I've loved you from the minute I first set eyes on you. Every second we're together, the more sure I am that you're the girl God wants me to spend the rest of my days with."

Using the corner of the blanket that covered his legs, she wiped her eyes. "God? I must be hearing things."

"Like I said, I've had a lot of time to think these past couple of weeks. Figured a few things out, one of 'em being that God's been pretty good to me." He tugged on her hand, pulled her closer still. "He put us together. I'll be thankful for that the rest of my days."

Cammi snuggled as close as the wheelchair would allow. She buried her face in the crook of his neck and sighed.

He took her face in his hands, forced her to look at him. "Look me in the eye and tell me you don't love me."

"Can't do that," she said, eyes sparkling with unshed tears. "They wrote some pretty good lines into those old B-movies, and I loved you at first sight, too."

Relief surged through him, thumping in his chest, at every pulse point. The future would be as rosy as her cheeks, brighter than the love-light gleaming in her eyes. "I think after we're married, I'll get me a dog like Obnoxious."

She kissed him long and hard.

"Is that a 'yes'?"

"Was that a proposal?"

"Yeah," he said, grinning, "I reckon it was."

"You 'reckon'?"

"Never been more sure of anything in my life."

Cammi got to her feet and pushed the wheelchair into the kitchen. After parking it beside the table, she stripped the tablecloth and walked toward him, twisting it into a rope, and tied one end to her belt loop, the other to his wrist.

"You tryin' to tell me something?" Reid said, chuckling.

"That's as far out of my sight as you'll ever get again." She winked. "Think you can stand it?"

He broke a piece of crust from the pie she'd baked and popped it into his mouth. "Somethin' tells me I'll muddle through...as long as the vittles are this tasty."

* * * * *

In October 2003, watch for

AN ACCIDENTAL MOM

by Loree Lough,
the next heartwarming installment of
ACCIDENTAL BLESSINGS!

Dear Reader,

When we hear the word *saved*, we not only remember the day we accepted Jesus as our Lord and Savior, we also think of everyday heroes, brave souls who daily set aside their own fears to rescue those in need, as the policemen and firefighters did on that fateful day in New York City.

Even the strongest of us have moments of weakness, when we need to be saved…from the pain caused by the death of a close family member or friend, the illness of a child, unwanted career changes, the loss of a precious keepsake. We need to be saved from the pain of being let down by someone for whom we care deeply. For a reason I've never understood, that pain is never as punishing as admitting *we* have transgressed.

Why, then, is it easier for us to forgive others than to forgive ourselves? Maybe it's because, having suffered at the hands of others, we know exactly how it feels, and "knowing" makes us ashamed to have caused that kind of pain in another. Or maybe it's because we can't imagine *God* forgiving our offense.

But that's where we're wrong; throughout the Bible, we read examples of the Father's tender mercy. So the real trick is convincing ourselves *we* are as worthy of His perfect love as any other sinner, from Eve to King David to Mary Magdalene!

"Wherefore I say to thee, your sins, which are many, are forgiven." (Luke 7:47-8)

That's the promise I cling to when self-doubt darkens my heart, and that's the lesson Reid and Cammi needed to learn—individually *and* together.…

If you enjoyed *An Accidental Hero,* drop me a note c/o Steeple Hill Books, 233 Broadway, New York, NY 10279. (I love hearing from my readers and try to answer every letter personally!)

All my best,

Loree Lough

P.S. Watch for the next installment of my new ACCIDENTAL BLESSINGS series, *An Accidental Mom,* on sale October 2003.

Love Inspired

TAKE MY HAND

BY
RUTH SCOFIELD

Being a single parent was more difficult than
James Sullivan had expected, and he returned to his
long-lost faith for guidance. But was his young son's
teacher, Alexis Richmond, the answer to his prayers?
And would their newfound love be strong enough to
overcome Alexis's painful past and give her the
family she'd always dreamed of?

Don't miss

TAKE MY HAND
On sale August 2003.

Available at your favorite retail outlet.